The Three Royal Sisters
Magical tales from
an enchanted land

Enjoy

Elena Sommers

Elena Sommers

The Three Royal Sisters
Magical tales from an enchanted land
Elena Sommers

Design ©Tricorn Books
www.tricornbooks.co.uk

ISBN 9781912821129
Published 2019 by Tricorn Books
Aspex
42 the Vulcan Building
Gunwharf Quays
Portsmouth

Printed and bound in the UK by CMP Poole

The Three Royal Sisters
Magical tales from an enchanted land

Elena Sommers

Princess Crystal's Wish and One Million Orchids

Seven-year-old Princess Crystal lives in a magical, covered-with-snow northern country called Bearland with her mother, Queen Snowflake. Her Christmas wish is to have her own royal outside garden with one million real orchids. Unfortunately, she realises that it might not be possible and starts crying. Queen Snowflake writes a royal proclamation, seeking for help. Some of her subjects – Winter, Iceberg and Holly – volunteer to help. Will they be able to plant one million orchids for the poor little princess and make her happy again?

Mary of Philiphia and her Seven Children

Philiphia is a wonderful country, with fairies, leprechauns and goblins. The rainbow sparkles behind the castle. Six gold leprechauns have secretly hidden their pots of gold underneath it, three on each side. I wonder, who will get the gold or even three wishes? The red ruby from Mars with triple magic mysteriously disappears. It then becomes unbearably hot. The King and the Queen depart in the direction of Mars to get a new stone, using their spaceship made of light. Their seven children, Prince Red, Prince Orange, Princess Yellow, Prince Blue, Prince Green, Prince Indigo and Princess Violet, would like to say their country without adults. I wonder if they manage to achieve it?

Rosella of The Darkness World and her Live-forever Potion

A powerful enchantress – Queen Rosella, who lives in a spooky castle in her country called Darkness World – wishes to make a live-forever potion. Her friends, Water, Fire, Gravity and Night, her talking pet, support her with her quest. To make a live-forever portion she needs a pot of the hottest lava on earth, a pumpkin, the ring of life, happy memories retrieved from 1,000 children and something else. Will Rosella be able to achieve it on her own or will she need the help of her friends?

Snowflake of Bearland and the Power of Teamwork.

The kind and beautiful Queen Snowflake lives in a country called Bearland with her six-year-old daughter, Crystal. Most of all, they like ice skating and dancing together. Every night, Queen Snowflake shows the little princess the intricate snow dance, which has passed from a Queen to a Princess through many generations. On Crystal's birthday, the princess falls backwards on the ice and hurts her head. She lies there as still as a statue. Snowflake worries about her. Her friends Northern, Southern, Western and Eastern winds try to wake her up. Will they succeed? Will the little princess be awoken?

Three Royal Sisters

The old King lives in a country called Philiphia with his teenage daughters, Rosella, Snowflake and Mary. Princess Rosella likes the colour black. Princess Snowflake prefers the colour white and Princess Mary adores everything colourful. After the celebration of the girls' 16th birthdays, the King asks each princess to bring him the biggest treasure of all in return for his crown. All three of them promise to bring him the treasure. Will they keep their promises? And who will gain the crown and become Queen?

Contents

The Three Royal Sisters
Magical tales from
an enchanted land

Princess Crystal's Wish and One Million Orchids

Chapter 1
Bearland

Once upon a time there was a snowy crystal country called Bearland. Everything was sparkly white there. A layer of soft fluffy snow spread all over the ground like a fluffy white carpet.

An ice crystal royal castle twinkled right in the centre like an enormous diamond, shimmering in the sunshine, surrounded by round bluey white, cosy igloos. The silver fountain glistened in the centre. Its icicles sparkled splendidly with their magic. Dancing, enchanted, sugary crystal, edible snowflakes fell down on the ground, silently bringing a spirit of Christmas.

The luminous Northern Lights – aurora borealis – sparkled bewitchingly behind the castle, creating a magical effect. Green, yellow, red and blue shimmering lights never disappeared from view. The Northern Lights danced in a different pattern and played a wonderful classical tune. Tall, vanilla ice creams appeared here and there for everyone to enjoy.

Talking polar bears, snow leopards, Arctic or red foxes and white rabbits lived inside the igloos, enjoying the coldness of winter. Their footprints scattered in all directions like a weird map, unravelling their secrets.

Tall, talking pine trees grew here and there around the kingdom. The trees were magically decorated for Christmas with twinkling lights by little, delicate snow fairies. Each fairy had her own tree to look after.

A kind and generous Queen of Winter, Snowflake, ruled there with her little seven-year-old, Princess Crystal. Queen Snowflake knew how to start and stop snow falling with her magic wand. She was a great dancer. She knew an intricate snow dance. Snowflake was able to magic Northern Lights. It was her favourite activity to change their shapes and colours. Sometimes, the lights illuminated in a zigzag yellow and green pattern. Sometimes, they shimmered in straight blue and purple lines. And occasionally, they twinkled in a swirly magenta and pink pattern, making it look glorious.

Princess Crystal was a charming little child who loved magic, Christmas, dancing, ice skating, creating Northern Lights and delicate flowers. Most of all, she wanted to have her own little outside garden. It was a very unusual wish for a northern princess.

Chapter 2
A Christmas Wish

Indoors, the castle looked enchantingly festive, specifically for Christmas. The flickering Christmas lights covered icy walls and the ceilings. Each room had a Christmas tree, beautifully decorated by little house snow fairies. There was no fire in the fireplaces. Instead, each fireplace had the magical Northern Lights. They flickered quietly, changing colours. White or crystal, made-of-ice statues of historical kings, queens, forces of nature and Gods, stood here and there gossiping about Christmas.

'I bet Christmas will be the best this year,' exclaimed Spirit of Christmas, lifting his icy arm.

'Certainly,' agreed the statue of Cleopatra, unravelling a white scroll of parchment. A delicate goblet of figs stood beside her. A scary, snake with a snow leopard pattern performed a zigzag dance.

'How peculiar! Every year we have the same conversation, just before Christmas,' remarked Queen Snowflake. Her long, covered-with-diamonds white dress swept the ice when she skated across the floor, and her white crown with diamonds sparkled magically in the semi-darkness. Her wise talking pet Arctic fox named Arthur gracefully followed her.

Princess Snowflake skated in and twirled three times in the centre. Her purely white ballet tutu with diamonds sparkled, reflecting the light.

'What would you like for Christmas, my sweet heart?' the Queen asked with a smile. Crystal's gorgeous face looked a bit dreamy. She twirled again on the spot.

'I would like my own outside garden with one million white orchids,' she whispered with a sigh.

'What a delightful wish,' agreed the statue of Cleopatra and swallowed a fig.

'You know the rules of nature, my sweetheart. In snowy climates they will die,' Queen Snowflake answered in reply.

'Can you break the rules, your Majesty? Just for me?' she answered with a sigh and the tears filled up in her eyes, making everything look distorted.

'I don't know if it's possible. I wouldn't like to lie. Please don't cry,' the Queen skated slowly towards her daughter and gave her a hug.

The little girl turned around and started to cry loudly. She sobbed for an hour or two and no one could stop her. Her favourite Polly bear wouldn't make her happy again. An enormous pile of Christmas presents wouldn't make her thrilled. The snow fairies tried to use the magic of Christmas to make her delighted again, but it didn't work. The large tears ran down her upset face and she stopped eating, even her favourite ice cream.

Queen Snowflake couldn't bear to see her daughter Crystal be so inconsolable. The last thing she wished for was to have an unhappy Christmas. She took a white roll of parchment and wrote a royal proclamation with silver ink.

The Royal Proclamation

Her Highness Princess Crystal is crying non-stop. Her Christmas wish is to have one million white orchids in her outside garden.

Anyone, who manages to plant one million orchids in the royal garden, before or during Christmas, and they survive, will receive a bag of silver crystals, a bewitched purple diamond and a chance to wear my Christmas diadem and meet with Santa.

The Queen of Bearland

This message was delivered to all households in the country by the little snow fairies. The only thing left for the Queen to do was to wait.

Chapter 3
Frost and his Three Grandchildren

A large, made-of-bricks and covered-with-snow house stood in the woods, among the talking pine trees. The area was very quiet. The cold frosty air filled their lungs. Massive snowflakes, made of sugar, fell down on the smooth, white ground quietly, creating a magic of Christmas.

The force of nature and northern wind, Frost, lived in this house with his three grandchildren: Iceberg, Winter and Holly.

Frost had the power of winter. He was able to turn anything into snow or ice or start and stop snow falling. Because he was a northern wind, he had the ability to fly and was able to transform himself into a powerful icy, brisk or wild wind. When he did so he had a huge power. Usually, the old man had a long, white beard, bluish white magicians' hat, a long white and blue winter coat and a crooked wand. His pet – a graceful, talking snow leopard –followed him all the time for company and protection.

His grandson, Iceberg, was 15 years old. He was a force of nature. His power was the power of icebergs. The teenager was able to cut off the icebergs from the coast with his powerful magic wand and send them to the sea to melt and float. He had a white, funky outfit made of snow and ice. Iceberg loved collecting treasure and nice-looking objects underwater and on the seashore. His brown hair gave him a handsome look. Iceberg's talking pet penguin named Sugar Lump was a real chatterbox. Usually, he skidded on the ice on his two feet, trying not to fall, making silly jokes.

His oldest granddaughter, Winter, was 13 years old. She was a force of nature, like her grandpapa. The girl knew the power of winter. She was able to start and stop snow falling, make a winter day warmer or colder and create talking ice statutes. Winter's blonde, almost white, hair was always in a bun. Her favourite Greek style, fashionable, short, white dress made of silk gave her a pretty look. She carried her crooked, silver wand far and wide. Winter's talking, white, pet cat was always beside her, stretching, yawning and giving her purring opinion.

His youngest granddaughter Holly – the healing girl – was almost ten. She was also a force of nature. The girl had the power of healing and was able to speak every language in their world. She was very kind and helpful to everyone. Holly had curly magenta hair, dark blue eyes and a lovely smile. Her favourite outfit was a doctor's white coat, white trousers and a thin golden wand. Holly used her wand to heal patients. She knew a lot of medical spells. Her beloved talking, white pet snowy owl, named Arctic, followed her as a shadow, giving her help and advice.

All four of them were sitting in their sitting room eating ice creams, when a snow fairy knocked at their front door. Their Christmas tree sparkled with multiple lights.

'Royal proclamation! For everyone to see!' she announced and gave Frost a chunky envelope with a royal stamp.

'How peculiar!' answered Frost. 'Thank you,' he chuckled and gave the fairy a silver coin. His spacious sitting room, covered with snow, full of peculiar objects made of ice, became even colder. They surrounded him, like three little children, waiting for a surprise.

'Open it grandad!' they screamed, 'It might be an invitation to the ball. How exciting!' They jumped up and down.

'Hold your horses!' He opened the envelope slowly and pulled the official scroll of parchment out and started to read.

'Her Highness Princess Crystal is crying non-stop. Her Christmas wish is to have one million orchids in her outside garden,' he read in an official voice.

'What a strange wish for an Arctic Princess,' Winter commented straightaway.

'Anyone who manages to plant one million orchids in the royal garden, before or during Christmas, and they survive, will receive a bag of silver crystals, a bewitched purple diamond and a chance to wear my Christmas diadem and meet with Santa.'

'Here is a royal signature,' Frost pointed. He lifted his head up. 'Do you think you are up for a challenge, my smart grandchildren?' he asked in his deep croaky voice. His leopard growled beside his feet.

'It will be tricky,' answered Winter in a low voice. 'I might do it because of presents.' Her cat Misty nodded and purred in agreement.

'I am in. I have an idea where to find one million orchids,' Iceberg answered and stood up. His penguin stretched his back, lifted up his tiny wings and waddled about.

'I'd love to help the little princess and make her happy during Christmas time. I don't have any ideas yet but I'll think about it tomorrow,' smiled Holly and her owl sat on her shoulder, whispering something in her ear.

Chapter 4
Iceberg's Adventure

On Christmas Eve, Iceberg got up very early. The moon was still visible on the horizon. He packed his white backpack with lots of useful, magical objects: his powerful wand, a diamond mobile mirror, silver spinning top, cubes of magically frozen food and ice burgers for his penguin.

The snow squeaked under his feet when he marched towards their garage to take his favourite snowmobile. His pet penguin jumped in beside him and Iceberg begun to drive through the snow. It sledged quietly, leaving a lengthy trail behind. In a few yards, he stopped and whistled ear-piercingly three times. Seven white polar bears galloped towards him, racing each other on their way.

'Good morning guys! Do you want to have an adventure?' he shouted.

'Good morning Iceberg. We are always happy to join you!' answered one of them.

'Follow me guys. We're going south.' The snowmobile sped towards the horizon, the polar bears running beside it. The graceful pine trees, covered with snow, reflected the sunlight. In a few hours, the heavy snow began to fall, obstructing the view. The wind blew harder and harder.

'We have to stop, guys,' Iceberg screamed through the wind. 'I must use my silver spinning top to find the right direction or we might get lost in this blizzard.'

They stopped and he took out a silver comb-like object with a handle and pulsating magic field. He rotated it fast and a bright blue pointy arrow appeared right on top of it. It showed them the right way.

Soon after, they reached green trees, peaks and grass. It suddenly became very hot for polar bears. They shook their white fur vigorously which came completely off. New, brown fur appeared instead of it.

'You look great guys, in your new brown uniform!' Iceberg laughed.

'Yes, the fur is shiny and lush and doesn't feel so hot,' one of the bears replied.

'Shall we set up a camp round here?' Iceberg yawned.

'Great idea, what about on this beach by the lake?' They all agreed and spent the night under the stars.

On Christmas day, everyone woke up very early and helped Iceberg change his vehicle into a flashy looking automobile. It looked like a racing car with funky black wheels.

It zigzagged speedily across the fields, hills and forests. The brown bears followed it nearby. Finally, they reached the seacoast. The seawater was noiseless, only ripples zigzagged above the surface. The sun was bright and the sky without clouds.

The bears worked very hard. They modified the car into a speedy yacht. Everyone went on board and they smooched across the salty sea towards the Orange Japanese island. The silver spinning top showed them the way. The blue bright arrow always pointed in the right direction. In a few hours they reached the island.

'Land ahead!' Iceberg yelled, pointing at it. The island looked almost invisible on the horizon.

The silver spinning top begun to vibrate and the blue light arrow gradually disappeared.

Everyone got ready for the exciting adventure on the unknown island. Especially Sugar Lump. He put his roller skates on to increase his speed.

Chapter 5
Winter's Adventure

On Christmas Eve, Winter woke up at around 12. She stretched and yawned among her fluffy, white snowy pillows. Her white cat Misty had done the same and she rubbed the cat's white, long, silky fur in reply.

'I like this state of hibernation,' she yawned. 'I don't want to do much today, especially this task. I wish I was a polar bear.'

In a few minutes she got up, dressed and put her make-up on. She looked very pretty. Winter went outside and skated slowly towards the castle. The castle looked especially festive on Christmas Eve. The enchanted Northern Lights flickered in a zigzag pattern with green and magenta. Winter stopped in front of the largest Christmas tree and shouted.

'Liana! Snow fairy! I have a task for you!' A beautiful, tiny, chief snow fairy wearing a white fluffy coat, appeared in front of her, carrying her magic wand.

'Hello Winter! Merry Christmas to you!' The fairy sat on the nearest branch of the Christmas tree.

'Merry Christmas, Liana. I need your help please,' she looked at her unblinkingly.

'Anything for you, your Highness, especially at Christmas,' the fairy laughed.

'Take one million snow fairies and ask them to bring me one million orchids from Gothic island across the sea.'

'Oh no, it will be tricky, I only will do it for seven enchanted white pearls.' The fairy flapped her wings.

'Yes sure. I will pay you,' Winter yawned. 'But, this job must be done on Christmas day.'

'As you know, with a backpack full of fairy dust, my fairies can fly pretty fast.' Liana hovered in the air, showing her strength.

'Ask each fairy to dig out one single orchid, put a protection spell on it and carry it back.'

'Certainly!' Liana nodded.

'When all the fairies are back, ask them to gather in front of the castle. I'll be waiting there and when it's all done you will have your reward.'

'Now I have to go! Goodbye!' Liana flapped her wings and disappeared in a puff of snow.

'Bye! Good luck with your trip,' Winter clicked her fingers and the snow started to fall deeper and heavier than before, obstructing the view and making huge piles.

'Purring, perfect job Winter!' Misty whispered, sweeping the snow with her long tail. Winter lifted her up and they disappeared in the white snowy cloud.

Chapter 6
Holly's Patience

Holly, the healing girl, woke up very early, even before the birds started to sing. She jumped out of bed and put on her favourite doctor's robe. Holly thought that she heard something weird outside on the snow. She looked through the window and saw nothing out of the ordinary at all. Holly jumped downstairs and opened the front door. The cold wind blew in her face.

'Anybody here?' she asked no one. At first, it was quiet, but then she heard something on the left. She looked carefully and saw a little Arctic rabbit, sitting by the wall. His long ears trembled in the wind.

'Are you all right, sweetheart?' she asked kindly. 'What are you doing here at this time of night?' The rabbit moved a little in an awkward way.

'My name is Snow. I injured my paw. Can you help me, Holly the healing girl?' he whispered in a shaky voice.

'Of course, little one. Come in. I will help you.' The rabbit jumped awkwardly in through the front door. His paw gave him a lot of discomfort.

'My medical room is there along this

corridor,' she whispered, pointing at it. The rabbit limped stiffly all the way to the door.

Inside there was a large white, brightly lit room with a row of 12 medical beds along the right wall. A huge silver table stood on the left, full of gold or silver wands, tiny bottles with fairy dust, roles of parchment and multiple bottles with weird writing on them. Three medical books floated in the air. When they came in, one of the beds wheeled itself in front of the silver table. Holly helped the injured rabbit to climb on top of it. She picked a long silver wand and pointed at the rabbit.

'Take 40 winks,' she ordered. The rabbit instantly fell asleep. Holly opened a pink bottle and applied brown liquid on to the rabbit's wound. This time she chose a golden wand and pronounced 'Heal self!'

A powerful burst of energy was released in the air. A white robot caregiver covered the rabbit with a white blanket, placed the bed where it was and sat beside him, to make sure that he was all right. The light turned down by itself.

'Thank you, Ann,' she said to the robot. 'He will be better soon.' Holly smiled and vanished in a burst of light.

Later that evening, a teleportation taxi arrived at their doorstep with a fox and her little cub. The taxi had three reindeers in front of it and a beautiful, ancient looking coach on the back. The taxi operated by modified fairy dust and it was a very expensive way of travelling. A wealthy red fox came out of the taxi, carrying her half-sleeping cub.

'A teleportation taxi has arrived,' Frost announced, looking at the window. 'Probably a patient, Holly sweetheart,' he coughed. The girl ran downstairs and opened the door.

'Hello, Holly! My name is Cassandra Fox. My little fox cub Alex is feeling unwell. He is hot and quiet, and I can't do anything about it.'

'Hello Cassandra! I will do what I can to help your little one,' she smiled. They entered a brightly lit medical room. One patient was already there. An empty medical bed moved towards the silver table. Cassandra put her baby on it. Holly took out her diamond mobile mirror and ordered.

'Lexa, measure the temperature, heartbeat and breathing.'

'It's rather high,' Lexa answered slowly and measurements appeared on the screen.

'Regulator normalise!' Holly commanded, pointing her golden wand directly at the child. A burst of energy erupted straightaway.

'Take 40 winks,' Holly ordered and the cute little one fell asleep. The medical bed wheeled itself back to its position and Cassandra begun to look after her tiny one.

'My poor Alex,' she sighed. The lights

dimmed down.

'I'll be back. He will be better soon.' She waved and vanished in a burst of light.

On Christmas day, Holly was busy looking after her patients. They started to talk and smile again. She was very happy for them.

Suddenly, a small splendid unicorn trotted into the medical area. He had light pink wings, a light green body and light purple hoof boots.

'Merry Christmas, Holly the healing girl,' he announced coming in. 'Merry Christmas everyone!' Looking around he said, 'My name is Cameron.'

'Merry Christmas to you, Cameron. How are you?' She shook his hoof.

'I think I have broken wings,' he said with a deep sigh. 'I can't fly anymore.' And he started to cry.

'Don't worry, sweetheart. Your wings will be fine. Tell me what happened. Why can't you fly?'

'I had an air collision with a golden eagle last night.'

Holly picked her golden wand from the silver table and said pointing at his wings, 'Fixate on normalise.'

A bright burst of energy erupted through its end. She picked her silver wand this time and declared. 'Take 40 winks!' And he fell asleep at once. A caregiver robot came to look after him. Holly smiled and disappeared in a burst of light.

Chapter 7
The Orange Japanese Island

The Orange Japanese island seemed peaceful at first. It was covered with maroon, turquoise, green, yellow, orange and white orchids. It was full of birds of paradise, butterflies and insects.

'Do you think this island is inhabitable?' Iceberg asked everyone.

'It looks quite quiet,' one of them replied.

Slowly and carefully they disembarked. They walked around the island, carefully searching for white orchids. It was difficult to penetrate through the tall vegetation, especially for poor little penguin on roller skates.

In a huge leap, Iceberg moved towards a white orchid and dug it out with his magic wand.

'We must collect one million of them,' he explained.

Suddenly, dark heavy clouds appeared on the sky, an enormous orange octopus came out of the sea and a beautiful Japanese lady appeared in front of them.

The octopus had six arms and two legs. It used its legs to support its heavy body. The arms moved around to catch its prey. Each arm had a mind of its own and moved in a different direction. Abruptly, it squirted a fountain of purple ink all over them, making them slow and sleepy. They could hear the thumping of the octopus's three hearts behind their backs.

An elegant Japanese lady walked slowly towards Iceberg. She was wearing a flowery diadem and a Japanese orange kimono covered with orchids. She was a force of nature and looked very cross.

'Do not take out my plants!' she demanded. 'Or I will capture you all and turn you into the orchids. My name is Suzuki Azumi and I have the power of plants.'

The last thing Iceberg wanted was to be stuck on this island forever and to be a white orchid plant.

'Sorry Suzuki! I thought this island was uninhabitable,' Iceberg answered in a hoarse voice.

'Plant it back now!' she commanded. With a gloomy face the boy obeyed her.

'Plant self!' He pointed his wand towards the ground and a beam of light appeared in front of it.

'That's a good boy,' she smiled. 'I will let you all go.'

She stared at them for a bit. 'But do not come back!' Suzuki waved her graceful arms in the air and the shape of the orange octopus disappeared into the green salty water. Then she said goodbye and bowed. Iceberg and the bears bowed back. It happened three times in a row and then she disappeared in a green misty fog. Quietly and carefully they walked back towards the boat and sailed across the sea.

It was difficult to go back empty-handed.

Chapter 8
The Adventure of Snow Fairies

One million graceful, white snow fairies gathered in a field nearby. They formed a flock of fairies and took off, elegantly, heading south. Because of the snow falling fast and obstructing the view, no one noticed their departure. They raised gracefully to cloud level and glided towards the sea. Snow forests, fields and lakes and rivers passed by underneath their feet with phenomenal speed. A good layer of white fairy dust on their wings gave them that haste.

Suddenly, the snowy surroundings turned into green fields, woods and blue rivers. The temperature increased and it became too warm for the fairies to fly in white fluffy coats. The fairies were too visible in white and could be noticed by strangers. So they landed, had a snack and applied more fairy dust.

'Colour transfer matter,' Liana yelled, pointing her wand into the crowd of fairies. Slowly, all of their outfits became summery and blue. The flock raised above the ground and sped above the woods.

Finally, they reached the sea. It was as calm as a millpond. The brightly red sunset reflected in the water at first. For a long time, the flock sped towards the horizon. It became darker and darker. Only the bright moonlight showed them the way. After a few hours they reached Dazzling Island, full of beautiful orchids and butterflies. The flock disembarked upon the island and slept overnight on a seashore. There was a scary noise on this island, which followed poor fairies all over the place.

On Christmas day, at sunrise, the fairies begun their search for the plants. They fluttered gracefully from plant to plant looking for the perfect white orchids. The buzzing noise became unbearable and one by one yellow and black wasps appeared in front of them. A nest of wasps circled around them, ready to attack. One sting could kill a fairy. Instinctively, they raised their wands and attacked the buzzing wasps.

'Freeze still!' they shouted.

With magic, one by one, all wasps fell down on the ground frozen solid, with a crunchy sound. While they were still frozen, each fairy collected one single white orchid, pronounced protective incantations and put it in a bubble on top of her head.

As fast as they could, they formed a flock of fairies and raised up from the ground to go back home. The seawater below was greenish blue, the waves splashed harder and harder.

It was almost dark when all the fairies arrived back to Bearland. They came straight to the castle. Winter was happy to see them all. The smooth, fluffy snow covered the freezing ground and sparkling, magical Northern Lights twinkled red, yellow and blue.

'Merry Christmas, Liana! How are you all?' Winter asked in a hurry. Her eyes sparkled with excitement.

'Merry Christmas, Winter! We brought you one million orchids,' Liana said pointing at her white snow fairies.

'Well done, everyone! Great job, guys, my snowy favourite friends.' She smiled and gave Liana an open silver box with seven white pearls, which dazzled Arctic magic out. Almost instantly, the air bubbles with orchids floated towards her. Winter collected them with her magnetic power and they surrounded her in a sublime way.

'Thank you, Liana! It feels so whooshing wintry great.' Winter clapped her hands and white dancing snowflakes appeared in a blink and surrounded her.

'It was a great adventure!' Liana smiled. 'Enjoy your Christmas! Bye.'

'See you later!' And Winter vanished in a puff of snowy dust. Only the Northern Lights flickered nearby.

Chapter 9
Winter and One Million Orchids

Winter stood in their snowy garden with her brother Iceberg who had a sulky look on his face. She was surrounded by floating white orchids, suspended in the air in their own bubbles. She pulled out her diamond mobile mirror and stared into it.

'Hi Lexa, dial my sister Holly please,' she asked quietly. And Holly's face appeared on the screen.

'Hi Holly! I have one million white orchids. Come and have a look. They look fabulous. I need your help.' A second later Holly appeared in front of her in a flash of light.

'Wow, Winter, you look so magical surrounded by them. Tell me, how did you get the orchids?'

'Thanks,' she squeaked. 'They were delivered to me by white winter fairies.'

Winter stretched and yawned. Her graceful cat Misty started to play with the plants. The bubbles bounced up and down like helium balloons.

'Magical!' the cat sang in a stretchy voice. They laughed and looked at each other.

'What is your next step, Winter? Are you

going to plant all of them?'

'I tried to plant one and I think it died. Can you revive it?'

'Do you think I am a Goddess of Life?' she laughed. 'It's already with the Grim Reaper.'

The plant laid lifeless and dry beneath their feet.

'I am only a future doctor'.

'Can you solve this problem, my sister? I can pay you, if you insist.'

'If you give me a healthy orchid, I can use a multiplying spell to produce an identical one.'

A single white flower floated towards Holly in the bubble. She grabbed her wand and whispered, 'Multiply self by two!'

A burst of light erupted from her wand and hung there for a minute. Two totally identical orchids appeared in front of them.

'You are a genius, Holly. I knew that you could do something about it. I have one million of them again,' she laughed. 'Thank you. Here is your Christmas gift.' It was a large Arctic white pearl. It sparkled with Arctic magic.

'With your help I can create my own ice golem, using this pearl,' Holly smiled. 'And it will be my friend.'

'I am your friend!' Holly's owl hooted indignantly, flapping his wings.

'I will help you, but how are we going to plant those plants?' Winter sighed.

'I think I have an idea,' Holly laughed. 'We have to ask our grandpa tonight.'

Chapter 10
Earth and One Million Orchids

When their grandad Frost came out in their covered-with-snow garden, he was amused by the scene.

'Winter, darling, you are going to turn into a plant yourself!' he chuckled. His leopard growled in reply.

'Grandad! Do you know anyone who can help us to plant those orchids in the royal garden today?' Frost took a few steps forward, thinking. His bluey white fur coat waved in the wind.

'I think I do,' he smiled. 'Earth can help you.'

He pulled out his diamond mobile mirror and spoke into it.

'Connect me with Earth, Lexa,' he grumbled and the lady's face appeared on the screen.

'Hello Earth, darling. This is Frost speaking. Do you remember me?' He pronounced his words loudly.

'Of course, I do. Merry Christmas, Frost! How are you?' she answered.

'I'm already for Christmas, but we have a problem to solve for the royal family. Can you help?' His leopard growled.

'I will be there in a moment or two,' Earth answered and appeared in front of them in a green misty mist.

Earth looked like an attractive African lady with gorgeous, black, curly hair. Her long, bright, olive dress covered with emeralds and green diamonds had a long train. She was a force of nature. Earth had the power of plants. She was able to control how tall plants grow, what type of surface they needed to grow and what type of nutrition they needed to survive. Also, Earth could start and stop earthquakes and mountain formation.

'Merry Christmas, everyone!' Earth smiled. 'How can I help all of you?'

'We need to plant one million orchids in the royal garden today. They must be strong enough to withstand snow and cold. Can you help us?' Winter asked in dismay.

'Yes, I can, but with a little reward.'

Everybody clapped and cheered.

'I'd like to go to the castle with you to see Queen Snowflake today.'

'Of course, Your Grace, come with us and enjoy our Christmas festivities,' Frost declared loudly.

The castle looked enchantingly festive on Christmas day. The icy walls glistened and reflected Northern Lights and magical illuminations from Christmas trees all around. There was an empty plot of land, opposite the ice rink, covered with snow, exclusively for the orchid garden.

'Winter, give me one million orchids please and I will plant them immediately,' Earth declared loudly.

'Certainly, Your Grace!' And one million bubbles floated towards Earth. With her gravitational power, she arranged them on the ground in a neat geometrical pattern. Then Earth pulled out a long, heavy, metal wand with a golden handle and directed an enormous amount of green energy into the plants. A green light illuminated from the wand for a while.

'Frost resistance maximum!' she yelled.

'Grow upon snow!' she shouted.

'Feeding from snow and ice!' she said loudly.

'White, Arctic orchid create self!' Earth declared finally, and the neat geometrical rows of one million Arctic white orchids were born. They grew straight from the snow and looked absolutely wonderful.

'Earth, you are a genius!' Everybody clapped, cheered and whistled.

'I was just doing my job,' Earth smiled and strolled towards the castle. Winter, Iceberg, Holly and Frost followed her.

Chapter 11
Princess Crystal and
One Million Orchids

Almost the entire Christmas day Crystal was crying. It was really hard for the Queen and others to see her so sad. The Queen decided to have a Christmas meal and party in the evening anyhow. She thought that it might cheer Crystal up.

Everybody was getting ready for Christmas in a different way.

The white castle fairies fluttered from room to room, carrying plates and dishes full of crispy roasted turkey, honey roast parsnips, carrots, stuffing and roast potatoes. They arranged cutlery with geometrical precision on top of the long tables, covered with white linen.

A statue of Mozart played violin in the concert area, together with an orchestra of polar bears and seals.

A statue of Cleopatra looked majestic in her Christmas outfit. She told everyone the most amazing stories from her royal life.

Queen Snowflake, Princess Crystal, the forces of nature and the Goddess of Life magicked the most magnificent Christmas outfits the world had ever seen.

Unexpectedly, Iceberg, Winter, Earth, Holly and Frost arrived at the castle front door. All five of them were escorted straight to Queen Snowflake.

The Queen stood in front of a large looking glass. She was wearing a crystal dress with diamonds.

'Merry Christmas!' she said after a long pause.

'Merry Christmas, Your Majesty!' The ladies curtseyed and the man bowed. All remained standing opposite her. The Northern Lights flickered magically blue and magenta in the crystal fireplace.

'Do sit down and tell me all about your quests,' her voice echoed in the hall. They sat on a white, semicircle settee and told her all about their adventures.

'As all five of you contributed to delivering and planting one million orchids for Princess Crystal, I would like to give you your rewards. All of you will have an invitation to our Christmas celebration tonight. Earth will have a bag of silver crystals with the power of growing. Winter will have a bewitched purple diamond with the power of shrinking. Holly will have a chance to wear my Christmas diadem and meet with Santa this evening.'

A page boy delivered all the gifts on an enormous silver plate. Everybody thanked him and the Queen.

At that precise moment, Princess Crystal came through the door. She looked lovely, but unhappy. The tears still glistened on her face.

'My darling, I have a surprise for you in the garden. Come and have a look,' Snowflake whispered and skated out of the garden door. Everybody followed her lead.

The garden was so magical. The Northern Lights flickered blue, red and green in a wavy pattern. The multiple Christmas trees flickered with their decorations. Crystal observed one million white delicate orchids growing out of the snow, especially for her, showing their delicate petals, beauty and Arctic magic.

'Thank you, everyone!' she squeaked and a huge grin appeared on her face. 'I can't believe they're real!'

She smelt and touched one. 'How magical! I have my real royal outside garden!' And she spun and twirled on the spot.

Chapter 12
Christmas Party and Holly's Wish

When they came back to the castle, Holly stood in a corner holding Her Majesty's Christmas diadem in her hand. It sparkled majestically with multiple diamonds, reflecting the Northern Lights. The Queen spoke directly to Holly in her kind voice.'

'Put my diamond Christmas diadem on. Turn it around on your head three times clockwise and say "Take me to Santa" and you will be in a dream.' Holly obeyed her.

'Take me to Santa,' she repeated and closed her eyes.

Everything spun in her head for a while and stopped. Holly appeared in a colossal building, almost like a factory. The room was covered with multiple colourful gifts and presents. Santa was in charge there. His 12 reindeers and teleportation sledge stood there waiting for him.

'Ho! Ho! Ho! Holly! How are you?' he grumbled. 'I am glad to see you!' He shook her hand vigorously.

'Hi Santa! It's nice to see you too. Merry Christmas to you and your friends the reindeer.'

'Holly, because you were kind and helpful for the whole year round, you can have a wish.'

Holly thought for a moment and whispered. 'I wish for all my patients to be healthy today.'

'That's a marvellous wish. It's granted. I would like to give you a little gift.'

It was wrapped in magenta paper. Holly unwrapped it and saw a book.

'Medical Spells for a Future Doctor,' had been printed on it.

'Thank you, Santa! I love it! Enjoy your Christmas. Goodbye,' and she disappeared in a flash of light.

The diadem brought her back to the castle. Everything spun in her head for a bit and stopped like earlier.

When Holly opened her eyes, she stood in the same corner, holding a book. The diadem was still upon her head.

'It wasn't a dream,' she whispered.

The Christmas party begun without her. She asked a castle fairy to show her the way. The familiar classical tune played around the castle.

Holly appeared in the dining area. Everybody had been enjoying their Christmas meal. She had never seen so many well-dressed people in one place. She took her place at the table and began to eat. She didn't think that she was that hungry.

The delicious turkey with stuffing, carrots

and golden roast potatoes was followed by Christmas pudding and white chocolate, vanilla and strawberry ice cream. The castle snow fairies served their food.

'It is the best Christmas ever,' declared Spirit of Christmas, putting a Christmas wreath over his head.

'Especially for me,' smiled Princess Crystal and glided towards the ice rink.

The ice-skating ball began after the meal. The Northern Lights and Christmas lights reflected beautifully in the magical mirror of ice. The kings, queens, forces of nature and Goddess of Life skated, showing off their talent. They glided, skidded, sped and twirled in all directions.

Happiness was in the air!

The end of book 1

Mary of Philiphia and her Seven Children

Chapter 1
Philiphia

Once upon a time there was a tall, magical white castle near a blue, deep, round and mysterious lake with mermaids. Pretty dome-shaped wigwams surrounded it, like icing on the cake. Short, smooth, bright green and silky grass spread softly around the castle like a magical carpet. A golden enchanted fountain was right in the centre of their garden, shimmering in the sunshine. Multiple talking, green oak trees stood proudly around the area, talking to each other and rocking from side to side. A large, arch-shaped rainbow never disappeared from the blue, bright sky. Even at night it was light and visible. It was always behind the castle. Six gold leprechauns hid their pots of gold under each end of the rainbow. Three on each side. It was their secret. No one had yet captured them or discovered the gold.

Queen Mary of Philiphia lived there with King Peter and their seven children. Small leprechauns, goblins and fairies lived nearby, looking after the woods and the gardens. Red, orange, yellow, purple and violet flowers covered the area, like a flourishing carpet. An orchestra of pink flamingos played their classical tune. White, fluffy sheep, goats and rabbits ran around the garden, for everyone to play with. Tall, rainbow, strawberry ice creams stood around the town, inviting everyone to enjoy them. Glittery, rainbow butterflies fluttered around the place, sending secret messages, like postmen for little fairies. Everything about this country looked enchanted as if it was a glorious paradise.

What possibly could disturb this peaceful haven?

Chapter 2
King, Queen and Lord Culture

King Peter had blue eyes and long, wavy blonde hair. He looked quite handsome. His usual outfit was a blue and red jacket, blue trousers and long boots. He was always on his talking white horse, riding around the woods. He loved organising the fun, fantastic birthday parties, masquerade balls, magical talking-horse racing events and the important leprechaun or fairy assemblies.

Queen Mary of Philiphia was a rainbow queen. Although some of Mary's subjects were goblins or mermaids, most of them were fairies and leprechauns. Queen Mary had a golden crown with red rubies, green emeralds, blue sapphires and purple amethysts. The rainbow halo surrounded her beautiful face in a gorgeous way. The Queen's dress was very long, silky and colourful. Everybody in the country liked their Queen, especially her friends and family. Every day she used her wand to make sure that Philiphia looked wonderful, full of life and colours.

Mary was able to magic the most perfect paintings of all, using her rainbow wand. Huge numbers of them hung around the castle, making it look incredible. Each picture had a little secret. It was an entrance into an animated colourful computer game. Anyone could go in and out of the pictures, whenever they wished. The first picture was a horse racing competition, where one could choose the fastest flying horse and win the race. Another one was a flying broomstick race picture game, where you could enjoy a broomstick flying race. The third game was a spacecraft flying game, where they could drive a spacecraft to Mars, the Moon or Jupiter. The fourth picture game was a jungle game, where they could start a jungle adventure and the wild monkeys would chase you. The children enjoyed playing the picture games. Sometimes they ran around the games separately or sometimes together, having a lot of fun.

Their tutor was Lord Culture. He was tall and thin. His long brown robes made him look like a priest. He had a loud squeaky voice. He spoke very fast, almost as if he thought that he wouldn't have enough time to give away all his knowledge. They studied magic, herbology, science and astronomy with him. Most of all, he wanted to be in charge. He disliked leprechauns and desired to uncover their secrets.

Chapter 3
Children

The oldest boy was Prince Red. He absolutely loved the colour red. He enjoyed wearing a red kimono and had a red, heart-shaped protective charm shield. Everything in his room was red. He had a red magic sword and enjoyed duelling with other boys. In battling, he was one of the strongest boys around. He loved eating meatballs, strawberries and increasing-power cranberry juice. His pet red kangaroo always jumped up and down around him. Most of all he wanted to become a king and protect everyone.

The second boy was Prince Orange. He was born with the power of fire. His costume looked like a walking and talking display of orange fire flames. His favourite foods were oranges, melons and magic orange juice. His pet firebird, with green, orange and blue flames, was always by his side, singing an amazing song. But most of all, His Highness loved fire itself. He enjoyed making scientific and magical experiments with fire, creating fantastic firework displays and night-time illumination shows. Most of all, he wanted to become friendly with fire people and learn more about fire itself.

Princess Yellow was the oldest girl. She was a clever, kind and gentle princess. Her long, voluminous blonde and curly hair surrounded her beautiful, smiley face in a graceful way. She wore a gorgeous, golden, long dress with many layers and puffy long sleeves. She carried her golden wand everywhere, casting rainbow spells. She had a cute little, talking leopard pet who was always by her side. Princess Yellow had an absolutely wonderful room. Everything in it was yellow or gold. She loved eating yellow magic apples, bouncy bananas, peppers and sweetcorn. Above all, she wished to learn about the power of the rainbow and become a real Queen.

The next boy was Prince Green. He was a bit shy. Sometimes he was scared to say his opinion. His favourite outfit was a green cloak and green robe. Everything in his grassy room was a different shade of green. It looked like a jungle. It was full of diverse plants and herbs. Prince Green was a vegetarian. Vegetables were the best in his opinion. He loved eating green energy salads, green peppers and curly cucumbers. His favourite activity was learning everything about herbs, seeds, trees, seaweeds and plants. He was always with a floating-in-the-air herbology book and a little, talking green lizard. The biggest wish of his was to become a famous biologist and to learn about the magic of herbs.

The fifth child of the family was Prince Blue. He was born with the power of water. He was an amphibian boy. He could breathe in air and underwater. He had both lungs and gills. Prince Blue had the ability to start and stop water flowing and start and stop thunderstorms. A talking pet dolphin floated near him in a magical bubble. He had a cool room with a swimming pool – everything in it was a shade of blue. All his outfits were watery blue. Sometimes he lived in the castle with his brothers and sisters and sometimes he visited the mermaids and Poseidon under the round lake. He liked the company of mermaids and spent quite a long time with them. Prince Blue loved learning about sea creatures, mer-people, coral reefs and underwater towns. His biggest wish was to become the king of one. He always imagined himself ruling under the sea.

Prince Indigo was the youngest boy. He was clever and loved magical stars. His favourite outfit was an indigo top and trousers covered with bright stars and a long indigo cloak covered with galaxies. He carried around a little telescope. A thick astronomy book floated beside him non-stop. His room looked like a night sky with multiple stars all over. It was a replica of a real sky. He was quite young, but he already knew many of the names of the stars, planets, galaxies and blackholes. Most of all he wanted to be an astronaut and become captain of a spaceship.

Princess Violet was the youngest girl. She had long, straight, red hair and bright green eyes. Violet was the witch of the family. She enjoyed wearing light or dark silky violet princess dresses, cloaks and bonnets. Everything in her room was a different tone of violet. Most of all, she enjoyed magic. It was in her blood. She had a violet wand, the fastest-for-her-age broomstick, a diamond magic mobile mirror and a little cauldron. She had a talking, stripy, slithering snake as a pet. It curled around her arm, looking creepy indeed. Most of all she wanted to become a real witch and learn about magic.

The royal children were truly amazing at painting pictures together. They had a lot of fun splashing magical paint around. Although each child had a different colour outfit, when the seven of them were together, all of their outfits magically turned white. It was a rule of light.

Chapter 4
The red ruby from Mars with triple power magic

One morning after breakfast, Queen Mary wanted to cast the usual rainbow spells. It was her normal routine. She quickly realised that she had no magical power.

'Something is wrong!' she exclaimed. 'I can't perform my usual magic!' she said to the King.

'What is the problem, Mary?' the King asked her abruptly.

'How strange! It's never happened before. Why can't I perform normal rainbow spells?'

He thought for a moment and suddenly asked, 'Do you think your Majesty, the red ruby from Mars with triple magic is still working and has enough power?'

'Let's check, shall we?'

They walked down to the dungeons and opened the secret room to unlock a silver case. The ruby with triple magic from Mars was missing!

'How horrible!' Mary exclaimed. 'Find the thief immediately!' she ordered.

Everyone was working hard to find the robber and return the red ruby with triple magic back. No matter how hard they tried, it was all in vain.

Soon, without magic, it became unbearably hot. The rainbow disappeared, the picture games turned black and white, the grass became yellow and dry, and big cracks appeared here and there.

'I will go to Mars right now and find a new ruby as soon as I can,' Queen Mary declared loudly. 'Prepare my spaceship!' she ordered loudly. 'I am departing now!'

'I'm coming with you!' the King announced firmly. 'You will need help. Lord Culture will be in charge.'

They kissed goodbye to their children and rushed into their spaceship. It looked like a large white sphere, made of light. The sphere raised up from the ground slowly and disappeared into the darkness. The children looked a bit sad after they left. They walked slowly back to the castle. It was very hot and hard to breathe.

Chapter 5
Fairies

The fairies were tiny, pretty, kind and caring magical creatures with rainbow wings. Normally, they lived in the woods. Every day, they were wearing their stylish, short, rosy dresses, carrying magic wands and little baskets. Each fairy had her own pet rainbow, glittery butterfly. These butterflies were like postmen for them. Whenever a fairy wanted to send a message to a friend who was far, far away, she used her pet to do it for her. Each fairy had her own talking tree. The fairies built their awesome treehouses using their magic. There was a competition among them. Whose treehouse was the best? There was a lot to do in the woods for the hard-working fairies. They had to collect honey, make magical dust using the secret recipe and help to pollinate the trees. They looked after injured birds, small animals and insects. Every day, the fairies fluttered from tree to tree in a graceful way, making sure that everything was safe and sound.

When disaster struck and the magic stopped working, fairies were the most in trouble of all. Although, they had their own magic, it wasn't powerful enough to save the woods. Their butterflies started to die. The pets were like friends to them and they were very sad. They were unable to send texts to each other and the connection was lost between them. Their favourite trees became dry and lifeless and it was impossible to be in the woods.

The superior fairy, Sophie, gathered all fairy folk around her and ordered them to go straight to the castle to be safe.

'The time has come when we are no longer able to stay in the woods,' she said commandingly. 'Go all to the castle in order to save your lives.'

Prince Red and Lord Culture were downstairs in front of their front door, when the fairies arrived.

'Please let us in, Your Grace. It's too hot out here,' Sophie said to Lord Culture in her loudest voice.

'I am not sure,' He answered quickly. 'There are too many of you. Go somewhere else.'

'I disagree with you!' Prince Red interrupted. 'We are here to protect them from harm.'

'I am in charge here,' Lord Culture answered, with an annoyed look on his face.

Fairies stood by the castle, thinking about what to do next. Prince Red rushed upstairs into his bedroom and locked the door behind him. He climbed on the windowsill and unlocked his window. Then he opened the window wide. The heat rushed into the room, making it harder to breathe.

'Fairies come in through the window. I allow you!' he shouted in a loud voice.

The little fairies rushed through the window, in tiny groups. Finally, the large bedroom became very crowded. They sat on tables, cupboards, floor, lamps and curtains. When all of them were indoors, Prince Red carefully closed and locked the window.

'Thank you for saving us, Prince Red. You are our hero!' They applauded and covered him with twinkling fairy dust. Anyone who had a shower of fairy dust became very wise.

'It's my duty!' he said with a smile. 'My parents would have done the same for you.'

The temperature in the bedroom gradually became normal and it was easier to breathe for everyone.

'I will go and stay in a different room for a while. I'll bring you some food and something to do.'

When Lord Culture finally realised what had happened, it was too late to fight. He thought he might have an opportunity later to have revenge and be in the spotlight.

Chapter 6
Leprechauns and goblins

They leprechauns were little curious men.
Usually, they lived in the woods in the dome-
shaped wigwams. They were as tall as fairies.
Their favourite clothes were emerald green.
Although each leprechaun had a pot of gold
in his possession, only six chief leprechauns
were allowed to hide their pots underneath
the rainbow. Those six leprechauns knew the
secret magic – how to hide the pots so nobody
could find the gold. The ancient spells were
cast on pots, after hiding them with minute,
tiny wands. The ancient legend proclaimed,
'Anyone who catches a leprechaun underneath
the rainbow will have three wishes and a
pot of gold granted by a chief leprechaun, in
return for freedom!' Many folks tried to find
the gold or catch a leprechaun, but it was all
in vain.

Some of the leprechauns were diggers.
They dug halls and tunnels for chief
leprechauns. Some of them, however, were
famous shoemakers. They made shoes out of
gold, silver, crystal and diamonds. They made
crystal shoes, flying shoes, dancing magic ice
skates or forget-me shoes. Royalty, Forces of

Nature, Witches and Wizards or even Gods bought those shoes, using their gold for special occasions. That's how the leprechauns, over the centuries, collected their gold.

When the magic stopped working and the rainbow disappeared, the leprechauns were in trouble as well. It was too hot for them to survive in the dome-shaped wigwams. The chief leprechaun, Charlie, gave his orders here and there.

'Dig out a huge tunnel, where we all can hide from the heat!' Charlie commanded.

The powerful beams of energy penetrated the dry and dusty ground from the diggers' tools. Along wide and deep tunnels, tiny rooms appeared slowly in front of their eyes. The multiple lava lamps hung themselves magically on the left and right side of the tunnel, giving plenty of light. All leprechauns moved on the ground in order to save their lives. Each of them chose their own underground room. The small animals followed their example.

'Dig out six pots of gold and hide them in a different location,' he ordered to the gold leprechauns.

With a beam of golden light, six gold leprechauns dug out their pots of gold, which had been hidden for centuries. Lord Culture couldn't believe his eyes. He crouched down behind the wall, trying not to miss anything.

'If I'm lucky,' he thought to himself, 'I might

get the gold and three wishes from those unwise leprechauns.' He smiled.

Each leprechaun grabbed their own pot of gold. The pots twinkled in the sunshine. All six of them walked in different directions. Lord Culture decided to follow one of them. The leprechaun walked fast with his heavy pot, stopping from time to time to have a bit of rest. He walked through the woods towards the mountain range. Lord Culture followed him at a distance. He moved as quiet as a shadow, trying not to make any noise. Finally, the gold leprechaun stopped in front of the large, dry oak tree without leaves. He put his pot on the ground and directed a golden beam of energy in front of the tree. Then he placed the pot in a hole and covered it with the dry soil and dry branches and leaves. Lord Culture watched him intently. He was too far away to catch him. The leprechaun pronounced a few enchantments and disappeared in a gold misty smoke.

When he disappeared, Lord Culture came out of his hiding spot, took out his brown wooden wand and read a few incantations.

'Excavate self. Appear pot!' he announced.

The drops of sweat appeared on his forehead. It became too hot to stay outside. Suddenly, the pot of gold appeared in front of his feet. The leprechaun stood at a distance.

'Why do you have your freedom?' he asked

the leprechaun.

'Because you didn't catch me!' he giggled. 'You found the gold underneath the tree. You're supposed to find it underneath the rainbow!'

'I can't have three wishes, but I can have the gold!' Lord Culture laughed and put the pot on his shoulders.

There was another tribe in their country, the goblin tribe. The goblins were greedy, wicked and cruel. They looked really ugly. They had skeleton bodies and large heads. Their yellow eyes twinkled in the darkness. They could hear very well with their huge round ears. Their skin looked brown-green. They lived in the mountain caves as lonely creatures. Every night they came out to hunt, like hungry hyenas. They wandered around the place looking for treasure with their pet rats. Goblins were the only tribe in Philiphia who weren't able to do magic at all. They were very jealous about it. When the temperature increased, the goblins decided to stay inside their caves and stopped appearing at the surface.

'It is nice and cool down here,' they sniggered. 'We have a big chance of surviving.'

Chapter 7
A secret club

In the morning it became even hotter. Huge dry cracks appeared on the ground. The trees became leafless and dry. All large animals ran away and hid elsewhere. Because of the way it was built, the castle was one of the coldest places around.

Usually, there was a good connection with the spaceship, which flew into space. However, this time there were no messages between the rocket with their parents and the earth for a long time. The children, especially Prince Indigo, were worried about them.

'We have to do something about it,' said Prince Red. All seven of them gathered around the table in their drawing room. 'Give me all your ideas, please.'

'It is easy,' said Princess Yellow. 'If we borrow a red ruby from Mars with triple power magic from someone else, I will be able to cast the rainbow spells and restore Philiphia,' she said firmly. Her leopard growled and yawned.

'Awesome idea!' answered Prince Red. His kangaroo hopped up and down.

'I will start the rain in the country to

make it more hospitable,' exclaimed Prince Blue. His dolphin agreed with him with echolocation.

'Potion power! You are genius!' answered Princess Violet, looking at him.

'When the ground is wet, soggy and moist, I will magically plant the green lawn, new trees and flowers,' Prince Green whispered shyly.

'Fantastic idea!' interrupted Prince Orange. 'I will contact the royal family of Lavinia and fire people to give us some help and advice.'

'Cool!' exclaimed Prince Indigo. 'I will try to contact Mum and Dad using all our space and magic gear. They haven't talked to me yet, but I know they will.' He sobbed and large tears appeared on his face.

'Don't worry,' answered Prince Red loudly. 'I will make sure that everyone is safe in the castle – especially fairies – without our parents,' he said, pointing his magic red sword into the air.

'Magic mystery!' answered Princess Violet, and her stripy snake slithered across the floor. 'I will use my diamond mobile mirror to call our aunt Queen Rosella. She's a witch like me. She might have the red ruby from Mars with triple magic. I will borrow it from her. What type of magic do you need?'

'It's health, power and protection, sweetheart,' Princess Yellow answered looking down at her. Violet bit her lip.

'I knew it,' she giggled.

'Amazing ideas everyone!' Prince Red said quietly. 'Let's keep it a secret,' he whispered, crossing his mouth. 'Especially from Lord Culture.'

Right at that moment, Lord Culture appeared from nowhere.

'What are you doing here, Your Highnesses?' he asked looking at them.

'Just playing, Your Grace,' squeaked Violet and circled around the room on her broomstick with a cheeky smile on her face.

Chapter 8
Aunt Rosella's talk

Soon after, and with excitement on her face, Princess Violet took her diamond mobile mirror. It looked a bit like a normal mobile phone with a handle.

'Hello Lexa,' she said into her mirror.

'Hello Violet! What would you like to do?' the mobile mirror answered her back.

'Contact my Aunt Rosella immediately!' she ordered loudly. A second later Rosella's face appeared on its screen.

'Hello my crunchy spider! How are you?'

'I am fine Aunt Rosella, but misfortune has come upon Philiphia,' she said with a trembling in her voice.

'What's wrong, my little enchantress?'

'Our red ruby from Mars with triple magic mysteriously disappeared. My parents went to get it from Mars and there are no messages from their spaceship,' Violet declared fast.

'Cauldron blast!' she shrieked.

'Philiphia looks like a desert. Can I borrow a red ruby from Mars? Come and help!'

'No, I can't come without official invitation and I don't have that stone any more.'

'Bad luck. Who does?'

'It's my old friend Water. She might land it for you, for a little reward.'

'Pumpkin power!'

'She is away at the moment, but I will send her to you in three or four days.'

'Aunt Rosella, you are the greatest witch ever,' Violet squeaked in reply.

'Don't tell anyone about our witch-to-witch chat. My sister doesn't like us to be friends at all. I am assisting only you. Speak to you soon, my crunchy spider.'

'Goodbye Aunt Rosella. I love you.'

Violet jumped on her broomstick and did a couple of somersaults in the air, with excitement on her face. Her snake performed a zigzag dance.

'Everything is going to plan,' she smiled.

Chapter 9
The boys' power

Prince Blue and Prince Green went outside together. The ground looked dry and brown. The multiple cracks spread out like weird spiderwebs in all directions. It was unbearably hot and sticky and it was hard to breathe.

'I don't like this,' Prince Green whispered to his brother. 'If we stay here long enough we may die.'

'I will start the rain right now!' Prince Blue said in reply. He raised both of his arms up to the sky, cleared his mind and yelled. His voice was strong and clear.

'The heavy black clouds bring your water here. The thunderstorms begin!'

Dark, scary looking, heavy clouds appeared in the sky. A bright, large lightning crisscrossed them right in the middle. The thunder rocketed, rumbled and roared, like a crazy lion. The huge, almost hot, wet and heavy drops hit the dusky ground with multiple force.

'It worked!' Prince Green screamed through the rain. The boys ran back to the castle.

After one day of heavy rain, the boys went outside to check the ground. The rain was still strong, but it wasn't as hot as before. The raindrops felt normal. The ground looked more even and the cracks had disappeared. The tiniest, microscopic looking plants appeared here and there. The worms, beetles and spiders crawled around the moist ground, doing their jobs.

'Brilliant result just in one day, but it's not ready yet for planting,' Prince Green explained to Prince Blue.

'Let's come back tomorrow and see the result.'

After two days of thunderstorms, the ground was completely green, covered with inch-tall, bright green plants. The temperature was bearable, not as hot as before. Some birds and more insects came back. The bravest and strongest of the leprechauns and fairies returned to their homes – they used their own magic to make everything look beautiful again. Prince Green walked around touching the soil.

'It is a brilliant result. We are getting there. Let's come tomorrow and have a final check.'

After three days of rain, the temperature was completely normal. The ground looked moist, soggy and rich. Everything was covered with a nice green layer of wild plants and flowers. All the insects and most of the animals came back. The horses, goats and rabbits grazed nearby on the rich soil.

'The ground is ready,' said Prince Green. 'Would you like to stop the rain now?' he asked, looking at his brother.

Prince Blue lifted his hands after this and ordered the thunderstorm to subside. Then, Prince Green took his green wand and directed an enormous power of green energy directly in front of him. The large beam of light looked powerful. Then he turned around and around, he wanted to cover the entire nation. The tall, talking oak trees grew slowly everywhere. The perfect green lawn appeared in the castle area and under their feet. The red, orange, yellow, blue, indigo and violet flowers appeared in the beautiful geometrical pattern. Everything looked as it had been before the disaster. Only the rainbow and the glittery, rainbow butterflies were not there yet. A little crowd of leprechauns and fairies gathered around them.

'Well done Prince Blue and Prince Green. Everything looks amazing!' everyone cheered. 'You are the real heroes!' The boys smiled, but Prince Green looked a bit shy.

'They didn't ask my permission,' mumbled Lord Culture with a serious face. 'They could have died.'

Chapter 10
Girls' power

Next morning, Violet went for a fly on her broomstick around the newly planted woods. She enjoyed the freedom of flying. The airstreams whooshed and swished, when she zigzagged left and right like a real witch. Then, in a few minutes she got tired and stopped. Suddenly, Water appeared in front of her, shimmering like a diamond. She was wearing a long outfit of all shades of blue and carried a little silver box in her hands. Water was a force of nature. She looked like a walking and talking waterfall. Water was immortal. In the same way, she was an amphibian. She could be underwater or on land as long as she wished. She also could control the water flow and start and stop thunderstorms.

'Hello, Princess Violet. How are you?' she asked with a sweet smile.

'Hello! You must be Water, my Aunt Rosella's friend?' Violet asked in reply.

'Yes, I'm here on a mission to give you a helping hand.'

'Can I borrow a red ruby from Mars with triple magic?'

'Yes, you can, for a little reward, my dear

friend,' Water smiled.

'Wizards' power! What would you like as payment?'

'Nothing special, my dear Princess. Just a chance to hunt leprechauns.'

'Yes, bewitched cats, it sounds exciting, but we need to make the rainbow first.'

'Here is the stone, my little princess. What do you need to do to make the rainbow up?'

'Thanks for the stone, Your Grace. I need to take it to my sister and we will do the rest.'

'Go and do it sweetheart. I will follow you everywhere under an invisibility charm,' Water smiled and vanished in a blue mist.

'Are you here, Your Grace? Let's have a broomstick chase!' Violet raised up from the ground on her broomstick.

'Yes, I will follow you my friend.'

In a few minutes they landed in the palace gardens in front of Princess Yellow.

'Hello, my sister. I have something important for you to see in this box. I am here with my invisible friend Water,' she whispered.

'Hello Violet and Water. What would you like to show me?'

'Hello, Your Highness,' Water whispered just in case. 'It's a red ruby from Mars with triple magic! Create a new rainbow please.'

'I will start my rainbow spells.' A smile appeared on her face. 'I must hold the stone first'.

She opened the box and pronounced a few incantations. The rubies sparkled in the sunshine.

'Curveball appear now!'

Then Princess Yellow took her rainbow wand and started to cast the rainbow spells non-stop. The outbursts of radiantly colourful energy pushed through with a colourful burst. The perfect rainbow with seven colours appeared behind the castle. The glittery, rainbow butterflies appeared one after another and spread all over the country in order to send important messages for fairies. The picture games became colourful again. The orchestra of pink flamingos started to play their classical tune. Finally, the scrumptious tall ice creams appeared here and there, inviting everyone to try some.

'Hats off to you, our princesses!' the fairies cheered from the formed crowd. The girls were proud like never before. Only their parents were not there to see their victory. Water was ready for her leprechaun hunt.

'They didn't ask my permission,' Lord Culture whispered through his teeth. 'I have a growing suspicion.'

Chapter 11
Water's leprechaun hunt

Water waited by the rainbow under an invisibility charm. She was sitting on a white fluffy cloud patiently waiting for the gold leprechauns to arrive. The sun almost went down and the castle walls glistened in the sunlight. Only birds and insects disturbed the quiet garden, screeching here and there. Water yawned and closed her eyes.

Suddenly, six gold leprechauns appeared underneath the rainbow, carrying heavy pots of gold. Water couldn't believe her eyes. She almost stopped breathing. She watched them intently like a lioness during her hunt. They put their heavy pots down. She wanted to grab one, but stopped. 'Not yet!' she thought to herself. The leprechauns pointed the beams of gold energy not far from their pots. A long narrow tunnel appeared in front of them, just wide enough for a pot to go in. They dropped their pots in and covered the gap with rich and moist soil and a layer of grass. Water carefully and quietly landed beside a leprechaun, trying to make no noise. She was ready to pounce. The leprechauns started to read their incantations.

'Preserve-self,' the leprechauns began.

Water leapt and caught him in a water bubble. She put him above her head. Because she was invisible, it looked as if he was floating by himself in the air in an un-bursting water bubble.

'What's happened?' he shouted.

'I just captured you,' Water said sweetly.

'Who are you, ghost or angel?'

'A beautiful lady,' she replied.

'Give me my freedom back, whoever you are.'

'No, sweetheart. I am making the rules now. Give me three wishes and a pot of gold and you will be free.'

'No, never! Forget about it.'

'Do you want to stay in this bubble forever, as if you are a wishing fish?' she giggled.

'Blast, bad luck. Have your three wishes, but not a pot of gold.'

'Give me a pot of gold and three wishes and you will be free,' she demanded.

The leprechaun took his wand and pronounced.

'Sure, excavate self!'

The pot of gold appeared in front of her feet.

'Good boy!' she smiled and put it in the bubble as well.

'Give me your three wishes. I want to be free,' he shouted. Water became visible and stared at him with her charm and glorious smile.

'Give me a red ruby from Mars with triple

magic as my first wish.' It appeared beside her in a floating bubble.

'I would like a genie in a bubble as my second wish.' He appeared beside her head.

'I would like a wishing fish in a bubble as my third wish.' The fish appeared beside her too.

'Are you happy now? I want my freedom back!' the leprechaun shouted again.

'Be patient, sweetheart. Thanks for the three wishes. Be free!' The leprechaun jumped out of the bubble and vanished instantly.

'Awesome hunt,' she smiled. The pot of gold, red ruby, genie and wishing fish were floating above her head. She took her diamond mobile mirror out.

'Hello Lexa! Dial Princess Violet!' And her face appeared on the screen.

'Hello Princess Violet. As you can see, I had a really lucky leprechaun hunt.'

'Flying broomsticks! Pumpkin power! Fantastic job,' Violet replied with a squeak.

'You can keep my red ruby from Mars with triple magic. It now belongs to you my little friend.'

'Thank you Water, it's very kind of you. It's a very powerful stone. I am truly delighted to be your real friend.'

Water waved goodbye and vanished from the screen. Only later Princess Violet realised that it was not a dream.

Chapter 12
Prince Indigo's determination

It wasn't unusual for their parents to take space trips to Neptune, Mars or the Moon. But it was unusual to lose all contact with them. Indigo worried about them. It could mean two things he thought – either they are alive and too far, far away for the signal to reach them, or their equipment is broken. Every day, since their disappearance, he visited their space observatory and control room on top of their castle. An elderly man, Mr Frenchman, was almost always there with his metallic, silver robot Luna Hover and typing tarantula. The sphere-shaped observatory had a large telescope in the centre and many brightly lit monitors around it. The stars twinkled on its ceiling.

'Good afternoon, Mr Frenchman! Any news?' he asked running in.

The typing tarantula typed speedily in front of the largest monitor. The man stopped what he was doing and looked at him with a sigh.

'No. Not from the moment I saw you last time.'

'I will send more messages today. Maybe they will see them.' Indigo sat beside the typing tarantula, in front of the large screen with the space map and started to send written, spoken, drawn, light and digital messages into space across a few galaxies.

'Hello! Where are you? Answer! Messages from home. Reply!'

He was determined to find his parents. He sent these messages again and again. At one point, the tears appeared on his face. He wiped them off with his fist. Suddenly, through his tears, he noticed their reply. The boy couldn't believe his eyes.

'We are here! We are alive! We headed in the wrong direction. On our way to our destination!'

He screamed with happiness, making Mr Frenchman jump.

'Congratulations Prince Indigo! You are a superstar. I told you that you will find them soon.'

'Where are you?' the boy typed again. In a couple of minutes, he received the answer back.

'We are approaching planet Mars. The time remaining – 16 hours.'

They looked at each other and smiled.

'What happened? How did you lose your way?' Indigo continued his questions. He was waiting patiently for their reply.

'First, we were attacked by aliens. When we tried to escape from their attack we got under a meteor shower. Then we accidentally ended up in the blue hole – a long blue tunnel-like place. It is an entrance into another galaxy. The galaxy we ended up in was stunning. It had millions of supernova-pulsating stars. The stars looked astoundingly beautiful, sending celestial magic. They twinkled with red, blue, orange, yellow, indigo, violet and yellow colours. The only problem was that we couldn't find the blue hole to go back. We spent a few days searching for it everywhere. It was only possible to see it from one angle. Anyway, it was an exciting adventure. If everything goes well, we will be back tomorrow at 2 p.m.'

After reading this, Prince Indigo asked all his siblings and Lord Culture to come and enjoy the news. Then he dived some more.

'Lovely news. Be safe. People from home. See you all tomorrow.'

Everybody was ecstatic to receive the fantastic news.

'Well done brother!' said Prince Orange, and gave him a high five. 'When they come home, I will make a perfect firework display to celebrate their arrival!'

His firebird started to sing a pretty song.

'You need to ask my permission. You are being rebellious,' remarked Lord Culture. 'It's wrong'.

'Sure, Your Grace,' agreed Princess Violet with a mischievous smile on her face and her stripy snake slithered towards him.

Chapter 13
Mars

The silver sphere of spacecraft headed speedily towards the red planet. From a distance, the planet looked like a large red pancake with orange, yellow and brown swirls.

'Finally, the planet Mars. Get ready for landing,' a captain ordered his command.

The spaceship penetrated the atmosphere of Mars with steady turbulence. The bright disk of spacecraft landed quietly on the red and crunchy sand and dust of Mars. Everything was a bit foggy and the visibility was low. The impenetrable sky looked brightly orange. Enormous, scary looking red mountains like great giants stretched upwards on the right side of the spaceship. A large, round bubbling volcano was beside them. An orange desert without vegetation, spread across the land in the opposite direction.

Three people came out in their glowing spacesuits. Each of them had a personal robot mars-hopper. The robots followed them all the time. The astronauts used their magic, musical roller skates to move around. Their task was to find a red ruby from Mars.

When they came out of their spaceship, they struggled to glide through powerful gusts of hurricane wind. The prickly, orangey wind full of sand blew, stopping them from gliding. They turned their helmet lights on and cursed protection charms.

Three astronauts glided in three different directions. The first one skated towards an orange desert. The second one moved towards a giant active volcano. The third one glided towards the mountain range. Their mars-hoppers followed them like their dogs.

The first cosmonaut glided through the crunchy sand, looking left and right. The orange sand of desert spread widely across the Martian horizon. The wind blew harder and harder, pushing him off his feet. He glided slowly through the desert without any luck. Exhausted, he turned back towards their spaceship. Because he couldn't see it at all, he went in the wrong direction and got lost. His helpful mars-hopper pointed him the right way. He boarded their spacecraft in the middle of the Martian night.

The second person went towards the large red volcanic crater. He glided smoothly around the crater, looking for the rocks inside the crater and outside. The crater had an ongoing volcanic eruption. The flame scattered crazily towards him. The temperature in his spacesuit began to rise. It became hotter and hotter to glide around it.

'Immune me from fire!' he screamed the protection charm.

Luckily it helped and his spacesuit became cooler, but no matter how hard he tried he couldn't find a single rock. Suddenly, a group of intelligent aliens circled him. They looked like electric, giant scorpions. They moved closer and closer ready to attack. He cursed them away, but it didn't help. In despair, he headed towards their spacecraft without rocks. The aliens chased him all the way back. He skated, waving his arms and legs against the wind. They nearly caught him. In the last second, panting, he managed to climb on board.

The third person decided to explore the mountain range. The brown-red mountains looked scary and uninviting. The small rocks rolled down from the top. He fell once or twice because of the rain of stones and the strong gusts of wind. Suddenly, he spotted a cave. Bravely, he went into the impenetrable darkness. His bright light illuminated a large hall with red and orange stalactites and stalagmites on its floor and ceiling. Weird-looking insects crawled around the floor. Very slowly, he skated around them. All of a sudden, he noticed something bright red. His robot stretched his long arms, reached and grabbed it. It was a ruby! The insects started to crawl towards them. Quickly, he checked its magicability using his wand. The insects crawled closer and closer. It was a real ruby from Mars! They came out of the cave and rushed towards their spaceship. The rocks bombarded them on the way. They skilfully dodged away from the stones. Then, speedily the man and his robot boarded the spacecraft and the perfect, bright sphere of spaceship disappeared into the darkness.

Chapter 14
Back home

The children couldn't sleep that night. They missed their parents a lot. They wanted to give them a great surprise. At around 2 p.m. a brightly lit spear of the spaceship landed in front of them. The entire crew of 12 people came out, wearing their bright spacesuits. The whole country, young and old, came to watch their arrival. Everyone cheered!

'Great to see you all!' waved the Queen. 'Our trip was quite successful, despite some complications,' she added with a cheerful smile. 'Philiphia looks wonderful again, as if it's never changed. How did you all manage to improve it?' She looked at everyone.

All seven of their children were trying to tell their stories at the same time interrupting each other and jumping up and down with sheer delight. When they finished, a scruffy looking goblin appeared in front of them. His oversized head nodded from side to side.

'Ruby!' he squeaked and gave the King the stone. The King stared at him and grabbed the stone.

"Why did you take it?' He bellowed. The goblin's arms and legs began to tremble.

'Sorry!' he squeaked. 'I took it. I thought I could work out the magic and be as strong as a king.'

'The entire country was in trouble because of you!' the King's voice echoed like thunder. The goblin shrank even more.

'Arrest him!' he ordered.

Two soldiers in red and white floated towards him, grabbed him by the arms and floated away with the greedy goblin.

'Outstanding job, dear children!' said the Queen. 'We all deserve a party!'

Everyone cheered.

'One and all is invited,' said the King.

'I am not in charge anymore,' remarked Lord Culture with a sulky expression.

The party begun straightaway in the palace gardens. Scrumptious food magically appeared on the tables. Busy robot squirrels served their food. Flying strawberry and raspberry cupcakes magically floated in the air. The jumping oranges, yellow bouncy bananas, green, curly, crunchy cucumbers, blue huge blueberries, indigo magic ice creams and violet stretching plums and aubergines appeared in front of everyone.

At night, Prince Orange organised his promised surprise. He prepared the most amazing fireworks the world has ever seen. A light of magical rainbow signalled seven times. A swoosh of twenty-five roaring red rockets blasted at the same time, with a noisy bang. A brightness of thirty-three orange Roman candles crackled fiercely in the night. A sparkly blaze of twenty-seven yellow Catherine wheels wheeled round and round in the middle of the night. A quietness of fifty-five blue sparkly fountains softly sent blue sparks into the magical night. A fire of six bright green sparkly stars twinkled with a swishing blast, sending the signal of fairy light. A shine of nine indigo roaring rockets went up in the sky with a bang. Finally, a shimmer of violet sparks erupted with a bang creating an enchanted sight. Happiness was in the air at this magical night.

The end of book 2

Rosella of The Darkness World and her Live-forever Potion

Chapter 1
Darkness World

Once upon a time there was a gloomy, creepy, cold, enchanted black stone castle surrounded by the impenetrable dark woods. The crooked bare branches twisted and turned in all directions creating a strange pattern. The black water of the lake, full of frogs and lizards, reflected in the moonlight behind the castle. The captivating, magical moving lights surrounded that castle – like stars in the sky distracting all strangers. The black flying horses grazed nearby impatiently waiting for their owners. The young, powerful Queen of The Darkness World, Rosella, lived there. Her unusual friends, Fire, Water and Gravity, visited her occasionally to make mysterious magic. The witches and wizards lived in these woods in the driving and talking wooden huts, which crept and squeaked all the time. A large, rectangular boarding school, made of brown bricks stood nearby. It was full of children who studied science and magic. The talking black cats jumped up and down the trees to show each other their magic. The wild, black talking crows circled round the woods creating a creepy chaos. All strangers were forbidden to come in or out, the country was under a dark magic spell. Everything about this country was dark and mysterious.

Chapter 2
Rosella

Inside the castle looked even spookier. An enormous hot blazing fire crackled fiercely in a huge fireplace in a tall, round, echoing hall. The creepy old spiders hung around the castle in enchanted patterns. These talking spiders whispered to each other, sharing their magical secrets. The black talking crows circled around the ceiling, screeching loudly in the hall. A chunky cauldron bubbled fiercely in the middle. It was full of gluey black liquid. A pile of bottles, flasks and jars with weird writing stood untidily on a table. They were full of different coloured liquid. A few scruffy old magic books were scattered around the floor. A pile of red poisoned apples, pumpkins and herbs were in the corner. A fat talking black cat named Night mixed a few herbs near the fire creating a cloud of dust.

Rosella stood near the cauldron reading a floating-in-the-air magical book and held her diamond mobile mirror. She was a powerful Queen of her country; everyone had to obey her orders. Her silky black long dress and black cloak swept the floor when she walked. Her diamond crown with rubies sparkled magically all the time in contrast with her pretty, silky black hair. Rosella was quite a strong enchantress. She knew many powerful spells and even forbidden magic. The thing that she wanted most of all was to be young and be alive forever. She wished to find a formula for a live-forever potion. So far, she was not in luck. Her old friends Water, Fire and Gravity helped her with her search.

Chapter 3
Mobile mirror

Next morning Rosella stood near the cauldron holding her diamond mobile mirror, Lexa. It could ask and answer questions, tell stories, show pictures, play music and even more. It looked a bit like a normal mobile phone with a handle. The Queen was always with it.

'Good morning, Rosella. What would you like to discover today?' asked the mirror loudly.

'Tell me, Lexa, what ingredients do you need to make a live-forever potion?' she answered.

'My knowledge is incomplete. You need five ingredients: two poisoned apples, one pumpkin, a pot of the hottest lava, a ring of life and something else I don't know.'

'Excellent, Lexa. We're nearly there. I have two ingredients already – pumpkins and poisoned apples. I know the fifth ingredient too.'

'What is the fifth ingredient, your Majesty?' the cat asked blowing triangle bubbles.

'Be quiet, Night!' she ordered. 'The fifth ingredient is a tiny bit of happiness taken from 1,000 children.'

'Where are you going to find 1,000 children,

Rosella?' Lexa asked in reply.

'Silence!' she squeaked. 'I'll think about it. Where is the ring of life?'

'It's at the bottom of the lake near the castle in the country called Philiphia.'

'Philiphia is the country where I was born,' she said into her mobile mirror. 'Ask Water to visit me. I have a request for her.'

Chapter 4
Water

A few seconds later Water appeared in front of them shimmering like a diamond. She was wearing a long, outfit of all shades of blue. She looked like a walking and talking waterfall. Her own golden wishing fish was floating around in circles on top of her head in a large, floating water bubble. Water was immortal. Also, she was an amphibian. She could be underwater or on land as long as she wished. She also could control the water flow and start and stop thunderstorms.

'Did you call me, Rosella?' she smiled. 'I haven't seen you for a long time.'

'Yes. Water, I have a tiny request for you. Go to the country called Philiphia and bring me a ring of life. It's at the bottom of the round lake. The mermaids protect it. The lake is right in front of the royal castle. I will pay well,' she asked impatiently.

'I wonder why, Rosella, do you need it?' she asked in reply, and her golden wishing fish twisted and turned in its bubble.

'For live-forever potion. Why is it your concern? I will pay well. What would you like in return?' Rosella looked firm.

'A red ruby from Mars with triple power magic,' Water answered in turn.

'No! It's the most powerful item that I own!' Rosella looked slightly concerned.

'Rosella, you will be immortal like one of us, a goddess or a force of nature,' Water replied in a dramatic turn.

'Fine, Water! I will give it to you when you return with the ring of life,' she announced. 'Now leave me alone.' Water waved and vanished in a puff of blue misty smoke.

'Don't drown, Water,' Night mumbled with an enormous smile, when she left and a red firework burst on top of his head.

'Shut up, Night!' Rosella laughed and the blackbird landed on her shoulder.

Chapter 5
Fire

Suddenly, Fire appeared in front of them. He looked exactly like walking and talking lava and a fire monarch. He had a dark red and orange jacket with glowing stones and long glittery boots. He knew the power of fire. He could go in and out of fire and it didn't harm him. Many things in his castles were made of fire. Two wonderful firebirds sat on his shoulders. The birds had green, yellow, red and blue fire flames in their feathers.

'Hello, your Majesty Rosella the Queen of The Darkness World, 'he announced loudly and gave her one of the birds.

'Thank you, Fire the Greatest, The King of Lavenia. It looks awesome.' She smiled.

'The bird's name is Flame. It brings luck to its owner, it is immortal and it has a beautiful singing voice,' he explained.

'I wish I was immortal, like you,' Rosella answered quietly. 'I am in the process of making a live-forever potion. Would you like to help?' she asked with a tremble in her voice.

'Of course, your Majesty, anything for your smile.'

'I need a pot of the hottest lava on earth, your Majesty,' she answered with a grin.

'Rosella, you are the one for me. I love you. Would you like to be my girlfriend?' He looked a bit shy.

'I have to be immortal to accept. Fire, ask me again in the future.'

'I will go and bring a pot of lava for you, Rosella, as soon as I can.'

They waved goodbye and he vanished in a ball of fire. Only Flame the bird remained in her hands. She stood there and looked at it for a while, thinking. The bird sung beautifully something nice. Then, her cat Night performed a magical dance with ten flying brooms.

'Bravo, Night! You are on fire!' She said goodnight and vanished in a puff of purple smoke.

Chapter 6
Gravity

Next morning Rosella invited Gravity to share her breakfast with him. Gravity looked like an old man. He had an enormous power to attract things towards him. Any objects, light or heavy, could fly in his direction, at his command. He was all in grey. Gravity was wearing a grey colour suit, grey cap and a grey shiny pair of shoes. A rolled-up newspaper was always with him and no one knew the reason. He was immortal and his talking pet wolf named Press never left his beloved master. Gravity had a deep croaky voice when he spoke. Usually, ordinary people were tired and sleepy in his company. However, over the years Rosella learned how to be friends with him. She simply treated him like he was her grandad.

'It was kind of you to invite me for breakfast, your Majesty,' he started slowly. 'What is on your mind?'

'Nothing special. It's just that I would like to be immortal like you. So, I am in the process of making a live-forever potion. I need a bit of happiness from 1,000 children. Can you use your gravitational force?' She sat there waiting for an answer.

'Awesome flying pumpkin cakes,' he said. 'I can help you Rosella, for a little reward.'

His wolf stretched and yawned showing his white teeth. One cake flew right into his mouth and he started to catch them non-stop, making everyone laugh.

'I would like a grey triple-power moonstone as my reward,' he said finally.

'Awesome! Deal!' Rosella squeaked in reply.

'How many children do you have in your boarding school, your Majesty?' he asked in his deep voice, catching another cake.

'725, with new ones.'

'I can take tiny bits of their happiness, with a pink memory stick, without them even noticing. The tiny spiderwebs of information will be collected from their heads into that stick using my gravitational force.'

'Awesome what about the other 275 children?' she asked impatiently.

'We will think about it later. Thank you for breakfast, it was fabulous. Press especially loves the cakes.' They laughed, waved then he vanished in a puff of silver smoke.

Chapter 7
Water's adventure

Meanwhile, Water arrived in Philiphia under an invisibility charm. Nobody was able to see her, even mermaids. She decided to explore the round lake first. There was a cute little mermaid city named Rocky, and Poseidon was in charge there. The city looked really pretty. It had a small shell-shaped white castle in the middle and a few small shell-shaped pink and yellow little houses around it. The mermaids and mermen, in colourful costumes, floated around it, minding their business. Shiny, golden and silver fish swam backwards and forwards beautifully, in a shoal of fish. The seaweed decorated the city throughout, creating an enchanted appearance. Water decided to search the town in order to find a ring of life, but no matter how hard she tried, she failed. The mermaids hid it so well, that even being invisible Water wasn't able to find it. She had to change the plan, and fast. She didn't want to use the last, seventh wish of her wishing fish to find that ring. It had got dark and because she was there for so long killer whales sensed her being there. All of them attacked her at once. She had no choice except to climb out. She scrambled on to the beach and sat their thinking for a few moments. The moon was bright like a pancake.

'I am not going back there ever again,' she said to herself firmly. 'I have to use my last wish after all'.

'Can you hear me, wishing fish?' she whispered.

'Yes, master,' the fish whispered back.

'Deliver a ring of life to my friend Rosella the Queen,' she whispered.

'All done, master. The ring is delivered to Rosella the Queen. It's time for me to have a new master. Who is my new master from now on?' the fish whispered in one go.

'Rosella is your new master, when she is immortal. You have to wait for a bit.' Water stood up and disappeared in a blue misty smoke.

Next morning, Rosella woke up and found a silver luminously bright little box with a ring of life on her pillow. A huge smile appeared on her face. She tried to open the box with her trembling hands and the simple charm, but nothing happened. Then she took her purple wand and directed a light of energy into the box. Finally, the box opened and she saw a little golden ring with a large ruby. A force of enormous power illuminated dazzlingly from the ring. 'I wonder what is its secret?' she mumbled. Then Rosella put a few different protective charms on it and went down for breakfast.

'Water is my true friend,' she thought to herself. 'She definitely deserved her reward.'

Rosella ordered her cat, Night, to wrap and deliver a red ruby from Mars with triple magic directly to Water.

Chapter 8
Fire's adventure

Fire arrived back to his country, Lavinia, constantly thinking about Rosella. His heart was thumping fast and he imagined her in his mind again and again. Lavinia looked rather picturesque and amazingly pretty. A red, tall, pyramid-shaped castle stood proudly in the middle, it was made from a volcanic crater. Smaller-sized, black, brown, orange, yellow, pyramid-shaped, made-of-volcanic-craters houses stood proudly around the castle. Four beautiful lava lakes were placed around the castle. The first lake was bright pink, the second lake was ruby red, the third lake was blindly turquoise and the fourth lake was deep purple. The surface of the country had orange sand, like in the desert. Hot geysers of chocolate were scattered around the town, inviting everyone to try some. Flying fire horses grazed looking for scrumptious cacti. Firebirds were sitting on top of the pyramids, singing or flying around, playing chase. Fire people lived there quietly. They were very interested in astronomy, science and magic.

Like their king, they could go in and out of fire unharmed. They had three sphere-shaped, made-of light-and-fire spaceships to visit stars and planets, whenever they wished.

Fire had something else on his mind. He took a fireproof pot and had a fast ride on his favourite flying horse towards a red lava lake. Then he decided to walk round looking for the hottest lava on earth. The lava bubbled and scattered flames. He walked right into the middle of the lake, using special magic not to be sucked in. Then he placed the pot, using its handle, into bubbling lava and collected some. Then he closed the pot tight and decided to deliver it straight to Rosella. He climbed out of the lake, and took a long ride on his flying horse. He couldn't stop thinking about her. Rosella was always on his mind.

When he arrived in her castle, she was in her large orangery or herbology room made of glass. It was full of exotic and ordinary plants. The room was very light and hot. The magical colourful birds of paradise were flying round and round. Rosella was wearing a long, silky green dress. She didn't expect to see Fire.

'Hello Rosella the Queen of the Darkness World, I brought you a pot of lava,' he announced loudly.

'Thank you, Fire. It's so fantastic. Not long until I will be immortal.' She smiled. They looked directly into each other's eyes for quite a while, holding hands.

'I love you Rosella,' he whispered.

'I love you too, Fire.' Then they had their first kiss. 'Flame the bird brings me luck.' They stood there talking for a few minutes and colourful birds of paradise flew above their heads.

Chapter 9
Gravity and his job

First, Gravity went into Rosella's boarding school. It was made of brown bricks. The classrooms were spacious, full of light and a lot of magical books and fascinating study material. The children studied the beginning of magic, science, chemistry, biology and astronomy. They also learned how to fly on broomsticks and flying horses during their PE lessons. Each child had his or her own little bedroom. They thought it was their second home.

Gravity collected the spiderwebs of happiness on his pink memory stick, during their lunchtime. Nobody noticed anything. Then he returned to the castle to talk about the next step.

'Here is a pink memory stick with some happiness from 725 children,' he said, and placed it on a little glass table, in front of Rosella.

'Can you possibly pull out 275 children from other countries around?' she asked and fiddled with the memory stick.

'Good idea! Of course I can. It might take a few hours, but I can do it today. It needs a lot of energy.' His wolf showed his teeth again.

'After you take some happiness from those children, I will turn them into black swans, to hide,' she said in her mysterious voice.

'Fabulous!' they shouted and started to work.

Then, Gravity took one of his grey flying horses and rose above the castle. When he reached the cloud level, he pulled 275 children out of their positions on the ground and placed them gently into Rosella's garden. After that he ran down on the ground and collected the spiderwebs of happiness. Finally, he had 1,000 of them on his pink memory stick. Then Rosella performed a complicated charm and weird dance and turned all the children into beautiful black swans and led them to swim on top of her lake.

'Fantastic job,' said Gravity and gave Rosella his pink memory stick.

'I couldn't have done it without your amazing talent, Gravity,' she admitted and gave him a grey, triple magic moonstone.

'Well. Awesome this little gadget will make me even more powerful,' he declared in a happy voice.

'Now I have all the ingredients for my live-forever potion!' Rosella smiled like a child. 'I will start making it as soon as I can. Please join me in the process.' She said goodbye and disappeared in a puff of purple smoke.

Chapter 10
Live-forever potion

That evening, Rosella, Water, Fire, Gravity and Rosella's cat Night gathered around the cauldron, talking about the process. An ancient, scruffy looking, brown magic book floated in front of Rosella.

'Step 1,' she read. 'Place a ring of life in the bottom of an empty cauldron.'

So, with his gravitational powers Gravity put a pulsating, full-of-energy ring of life right in the middle of the empty cauldron.

'Do you know that the ring of life increases everyone's life in the country for 500 years?' he asked everyone.

'This is a nice surprise for my people,' Rosella answered quietly.

'Step 2. Pour in some water and let it boil for a minute,' she read. 'Then place a large pumpkin and two poisoned apples in it.'

Water added some water. Night put in apples and pumpkins. Fire set up a nice steady fire underneath.

'Step 3. Place a pot of the hottest lava on earth into the mixture and boil for six hours.'

Fire added lava and they had a long time

to wait. It was almost morning when it was time for the next step.

'Step 4. Sprinkle the positive energy, collected from 1,000 children into the mixture,' Rosella read the instructions and then sprinkled the memories all over.

'Step 5. If the mixture turns into a nice red colour you can cool it down and drink it,' Rosella read further.

'It's red enough for me,' said Gravity.

Water took the mixture and gently cooled it down. Then she poured it into a crystal glass.

'Are you ready, your Majesty?' she asked the Queen.

'Yes, I am unquestionably ready. I have waited for this moment my entire life.'

She took a crystal glass raised it, said cheers and drank almost everything before stumbling backwards. The glass fell out of her hand, but didn't break, just spilled some liquid. Rosella nearly lost consciousness. Gravity put her on a settee. All the voices in her head were distant and unreal. In a few minutes she felt stronger and stronger. Then she understood the question and opened her eyes.

'Are you all right, my love?' Fire asked loudly. 'Congratulations for being immortal.'

'Yes, I feel so strong and powerful, like

never before.'

She stood up and walked towards him. Suddenly, her cat, Night, jumped across the room and licked the rest of the potion.

'Naughty boy!' Rosella said in her croaky voice and smiled.

'Please come to my castle everyone to celebrate!' Fire proclaimed loudly.

Chapter 11
Marriage proposal

Rosella looked especially beautiful at that moment. She was wearing a maroon, silky dress, which swept on the floor when she walked. Her eyes sparkled mysteriously and a huge smile was always on her face. They all appeared instantaneously in Fire's pyramid-shaped Royal Hall. It had golden walls and a red slippery marble floor. A large fire burned in a red marble fireplace. The multiple talking lit candles and mirrors decorated the room. A round, white table for four was prepared exactly in the middle. Five beautiful firebirds with pink, red, green and blue fire-flamed feathers flew around the Royal Hall, singing sweetly. Four robot penguins served breakfast, waddling from side to side. Four immortal people sat around the table, comfortably. The King Fire stood up and gave his royal speech.

'Firstly, we are all gathered here to congratulate Rosella the Queen of The Darkness World with becoming immortal.' Everyone cheered.

'Then, I would like to ask Rosella to become the Queen of Lavinia, my wife, mother of my children, my Queen and share an eternity together. Rosella would you like to marry me?'

'Yes! I do, your Majesty.' He walked across the room and put a white luminous ring on her finger.

'This ring is made of light,' he explained. 'It is the most expensive ring in our galaxy. It can be white or change colour to any colour of the rainbow at your command.'

'Thank you Fire the Greatest. It is the best day of my life!' She smiled and gave him a hug.

'Congratulations, your Majesty! Here is my wedding present for you. It is a wishing fish. It has seven wishes. After that it has to change master,' Water said smiling and gave Rosella her gift.

'Thank you! It's marvellous. I don't even know what to wish for,' Rosella answered with a grin and gave her a quick glance.

'This is a magical, infinite energy stone,' said Gravity and took out a little grey box. 'It has so much energy, that it can help your spaceship travel faster than the speed of light.' He gave it to Fire.

'Wow!' His eyes round. 'Thank you, Gravity! I have never seen one before.' They shook hands. 'It will definitely become useful, when I take my future wife on my next space trip.' He smiled.

Then, Rosella's cat Night showed his dance routine with ten broomsticks. Press caught a few cakes, making everyone laugh. Everyone enjoyed themselves during this celebration.

Suddenly, Rosella's mobile mirror spoke loudly.

'The parents and guardians of the children arrived at your castle, destroyed protection charms and demanded their children. Your sisters Snowflake of Bearland and Mary of Philiphia brought them there.'

Rosella stood up, said thank you and goodbye and disappeared in purple smoke.

Chapter 12
Parents and guardians

Rosella put a few extra charms inside the castle and appeared on her royal balcony, wearing a purple dress and a pointy hat. She had a purple wand with her just in case.

'Crazy witch! Where are our children? Give them back or we will destroy your castle!' the people shouted from the crowd.

'Your kids are here!' she started. 'You can destroy my castle, but you can't destroy me because I am immortal.' Her voice sounded strong and loud.

'Liar! Give them back!' someone yelled.

'As you wish!' She waved her right hand gracefully and a flock of black swans landed on the ground, beside their parents and turned straight back into kids. All of them except one.

'Why did you come here Snowflake and Mary?' Rosella asked her sisters in a loud voice.

'To collect Princess Crystal, Prince Orange and Princess Yellow,' Snowflake replied straightaway.

'What a stupid question. I thought you were clever. Why did you take them?' Mary answered too.

'Do you know what my beloved sisters, I am getting married, but not inviting either of you.'

'Nobody needs your weird invitations,' Snowflake answered with a trembling voice.

'Go! Now! All of you out of my land and never return, if you don't want a serious conflict.'

Everybody gradually disappeared. Rosella stood on the balcony for a long time like a statue. In the bottom of her heart she felt sad about arguing with her sisters, but she didn't show it. The three of them used to run around the castle laughing, when they were little kids.

All of a sudden, she noticed a single black swan left behind. She came down to the bird and turned it into a child. It was a little mermaid girl.

'What is your name, my dear?' she asked the child.

'Adele Lobster, your Majesty,' she answered bravely back.

'Where are your parents, my poor little child?' the Queen asked again.

'They died when I was a baby. I grew up in an orphanage with all the other kids.'

'Maybe your principal is looking for you everywhere?'

'No, she hates me,' the child replied and

started to cry.

'I have an idea,' Rosella smiled. 'Would you like to stay in my boarding school? I can become your parent forever. What do you think about that?'

'Sounds amazing!' She jumped up and down. 'Thank you, your Majesty. You are truly the best.'

Rosella took Adele's hand and walked all the way to her boarding school. She gave the child to the principal and made sure that everything was done for her in the best possible way. Adele received her own little bedroom and was shown around the school.

Chapter 13
Wedding day

They decided to have their wedding day on a little island in the middle of a pink lava lake. The sky looked purple, contrasting with the pink quiet water. The pink flamingos floated gracefully around the lake. The island had a little golden pyramid-shaped castle in the middle of the perfect green lawn. The numerous firebirds flew around the island, singing beautiful melodies. The chocolate geysers were here and there, inviting everyone to enjoy. A few tables were outside full of scrumptious, exotic food. There were jumping magic jellies, flying pumpkin pies, mini chocolate broomsticks and pumpkin happiness potion. A few cute robot penguins served their meals.

The ballroom had golden walls and delicate mirrors throughout and a pink marble floor. The wedding guests looked absolutely fantastic with golden, silver, purple and yellow dresses and suits. They talked to each other quietly, waiting for the ceremony to begin.

The King Fire was wearing a golden jacket with rubies, a golden royal crown, red trousers and golden long boots. All his family and relations, forces of nature, one god, two angels, witches and wizards were already there. Only the bride was missing.

Finally, she appeared wearing a golden dress with red and yellow flames throughout with a long train behind her. Three little bridesmaids in red helped to carry the train. One of them was Adele. Rosella looked absolutely gorgeous. Her royal crown sparkled with rubies and diamonds, in contrast with her black hair. She walked towards the King with Gravity. He was wearing a silver suit and a silver air cylinder. The firebirds sung a wedding song.

'I Fire, the King of Lavinia, take you Rosella, the Queen of The Darkness World, to be my lawful wedded wife, in sickness and in health for eternity,' he said proudly.

'I Rosella, the Queen of The Darkness World, take you King Fire of Lavinia to be my lawful wedded husband, in sickness and in health for eternity,' she answered him in her croaky voice.

'I pronounce you husband and wife. You may kiss the bride,' a white angel said loudly. They exchanged the rings. Than they had a long passionate kiss. The tons of colourful confetti fell down on the ground for a long time. Then they had an amazing wedding breakfast celebration. The wedding night finished with a broomstick-flying disco under the bright full moon and mysterious stars.

They all lived happily ever after

The end of book 3

The Power of Teamwork

Chapter 1
Bearland

Once upon a time there was a white, magical country called Bearland. Snowflake was the Queen there. A tall, magic, sugary crystal, white, snowy-iced castle stood proudly, surrounded by the blueish white, round igloos.

A thick, fluffy blanket of snow covered beautifully the trees and the ground. The tall arches of vanilla ice cream in the crystal dishes stood there around the town inviting everyone to have a bite.

The polar bears, snow leopards, white rabbits and the Arctic foxes slowly walked around the area minding their business. The large, magical, glittery snowflakes made of sugar fell smoothly and silently on the ground, creating the enchanted patterns of winter.

Chapter 2
The Snow Dance

Snowflake of Bearland was a very powerful Queen of winter. She could start and stop snow falling. She knew the old secret of the intricate snow dance. Every evening she went right to the top of her enchanted castle to say hello to one, two, three or even all four of her friends, the Winds of the Nature, and perform the secret, powerful dance of the snow.

No one else was allowed to watch her except her stunningly sweet six-year-old daughter Crystal, because the secret passed only from the Queen to the Princess.

The dance had many difficult pirouettes, twirls and leaps. Although Crystal danced with her mum many times, she wasn't ready to do it on her own yet.

Chapter 3
Dancing on Ice

The time came for Crystal's seventh birthday. The Queen decided to organise a masquerade ice-skating ball. Everyone had to magic the most amazing and sparkly charming costume.

The lights magically flickered on the round ice rink.

The ice looked like a smooth mirror, reflecting everything around. The skating ball was amazing. Everyone showed off their best skating skills. Crystal was trying her hardest.

She wanted to impress everyone. She twirled and twirled, glided and slid. Suddenly, her foot twisted and she fell backwards on the ground and hurt her head. Everybody gasped. She laid silently on the floor, her eyes and even her toes did not move.

'Crystal, what's wrong?' the Queen exclaimed into the silence. Only a bird screeched in reply.

The Queen walked towards her daughter and cast a powerful medical spell. Nothing happened. Her daughter laid as still as a statue. They gently brought her into her delicate white bedroom to sleep in her cute little bed. Crystal's beloved bear Polly was sitting nearby, looking after her favourite friend.

Chapter 4
Northern Wind Frost

The party finished abruptly. Snowflake was worried about her daughter. She walked backwards and forwards non-stop.

'Please help!' She announced. 'Whoever brings my daughter back will receive a bag of silver.'

Silver was the most expensive metal in Bearland.

'I would like to help!', said Northern Wind firmly. His name was Frost. He was the coldest wind ever. He had a long white beard and looked very old. He had a pet snow leopard, who followed him everywhere like a dog. He was wearing a fluffy, long light blue and white robe, which swept across the floor.

When they walked into Crystal's bedroom the Queen asked with a sigh, 'My spell didn't help. I wonder why?'

'Was she wearing magic ice skates?' he asked in reply.

'Yes,' she sobbed, in trying not to cry. 'We all know that a pair of magic ice skates protects you from falling. It's not a natural cause.'

'She must be under a curse. I can try the healing spell of Frost. It might wake her up.'

He raised his crooked wand and cast a blue misty spell directly onto the child.

It felt like time had stopped for a second. Ice crystals cracked around the room and crumbled into pieces on a white marble floor. It suddenly became extremely cold for Polly Bear and the Queen.

The princess was as cold as ice cream.

Chapter 5
Southern Wind Auster

Southern Wind decided to help. His name was Auster. He looked exactly like an African prince. He had lilac, purple and lime feathers in his crown, a brightly coloured feathery costume with rubies, grassy flying shoes and a heavy golden chain on his neck. His feathery wand was connected to his bracelet with a golden chain. He had a pet hummingbird behind his back.

'I think the hummingbird healing spell might wake Crystal up,' he said with a smile and performed a strange dance.

The sounds of drums filled the air. The warm African air filled the room for a moment, the walls started to melt. Everything around them was vibrating like an old alarm clock. Crystal opened her eyes for a second and fell asleep again.

'Thank you for trying,' said the Queen with a smile. 'Would anyone else like to have a try?'

Chapter 6
Eastern Wind Gail

Eastern Wind looked like a sea captain. His name was Gail. He was wearing a navy-blue captain's hat and a navy-blue costume with white buttons. He had a wave-shaped wand and a talking golden box of treasure. Rubies, diamonds, sapphires and pearls magically glittered out of his treasure chest arguing with one another. His pet parrot squawked loudly something funny.

'Ahoy there matey! I can try my sea healing spell,' he said rocking from side to side.

Everyone felt a fresh sea breeze and salty seawater on their faces, when he cast his spell. The castle rocked from side to side in a wavy motion. The child stretched and smiled, but didn't wake up.

'Thank you, thank you captain Gail', said the Queen. 'Would anyone like to have a try? She almost awoke.'

Chapter 7
Western Wind Anthony

Western Wind wanted to help as well. His name was Anthony. He looked like a young boy. He was the youngest brother of all four Winds of the Nature. He knew the power of the hurricane. He was wearing a metallic silver robe, a thin light-blue cloak and a pair of shiny boots. A talking golden eagle followed him far and wide.

Everything was shaking and the objects went flying around when he cast his healing hurricane spell, using his invisible wand. Crystal woke up for a moment and looked at everyone. Then she fell asleep again when the spell stopped working.

'It nearly worked!' he said with a giggle.

'Thank you for trying Western Wind,' she said with a sigh.

Chapter 8
Queen Mary of Philiphia

Then her sister Mary, the Queen of Philiphia, decided to help. She knew the power of rainbows and was quite a powerful Queen.

Mary was wearing a multicoloured dress and rainbow tiara.

'I can try a rainbow healing spell for my niece. It might help to wake her up,' she said softly, raising her colourful wand.

Suddenly, everything went radiantly colourful and a kaleidoscope of colours pushed through with a burst. Crystal stretched and nearly woke up altogether.

Snowflake looked at her with hope. She had the army of polar bears, the police force of foxes, snowmen and snow maidens at her command. But no one could help to wake her daughter up.

Chapter 9
Rosella, the Queen of
The Darkness World

Suddenly, Rosella her older sister, The Queen of The Darkness World, appeared in front of them, surrounded by the talking crows.

'I am the strongest and the most powerful here!' she cackled. 'Nobody can break my spell'.

'Rosella, what are you doing here?' Snowflake asked firmly.

'Why didn't you invite me to this birthday party?' the witch asked in reply. 'I wanted to be here like everyone else,' she cried.

'I simply forgot,' Snowflake said with a sigh.

'No, you didn't,' she said in reply.

'It's you who cast a spell on my daughter.'

'Good, I guess you always were clever! Now undo it!' she said with a smirk.

'Why did you do it? She's your niece.'
'The power of snow dance is the reason. I don't want Crystal to learn it. I cursed her when I was a bird.'

'Go and never come back as a queen or a bird,' Snowflake screamed. She wanted to be heard. The witch disappeared in a path of purple smoke.

Chapter 10
Polly bear

'I can help,' squeaked Polly Bear.

Everyone looked down at her in surprise.

'You can try your spells altogether. It might help to wake up my best friend after all.'

'Good idea!' said Snowflake with a smile.

They all conjured a spell altogether. The ground shook and rocked from side to side. The castle walls started to crumble. Everything was flying round and round. It was hot, cold, damp and colourful at the same time. At one point Crystal walked up and followed her mother. She gave her a cuddle.

'You are awake!' she screamed through the wind.

Everyone was happy like never before.

'Thank you for waking me up everybody,' Crystal said hugging Polly a lot.

'Great job everybody. It is the power of teamwork. Polly Bear you deserve a special gift. Have this bag of silver for saving the Princess. Let's all have a party without the witch.' They had a huge party to rejoice altogether with magical ice creams, jumping marshmallows, edible, sweet snow, flying white chocolate cream cakes and yummy, scrummy vanilla yoghurt.

Everyone enjoyed the cool celebration.

Everyone was happy forever after.

The end of book 4

Three Royal Sisters

Chapter 1

Once upon a time there was a very tall white castle near the blue, round lake. It was surrounded by green fields and rolling hills that nearly touched the clouds. The old King of Philiphia lived there with his three beautiful teenage daughters: Rosella, Snowflake and Mary. He loved them all dearly.

His oldest daughter, Rosella, was amazing at dark magic. She was strong and powerful and loved the colour black.

His second daughter, Snowflake, was great at white magic. Snowflake enjoyed winter, snow and ice. She was gentle and generous and loved the colour white.

His youngest daughter, Mary, knew the power of rainbows. She was excellent at painting and adored bright colours.

Chapter 2

When Rosella turned sixteen, the King organised an amazing birthday party especially for his first daughter. Rosella invited one hundred witches and wizards to celebrate. The party colour was black. Throughout the party they had spicy, jumping magic jellies, chocolate magic wands, pumpkin juice and pumpkin pies. Then they had a broomstick disco and flying race.

The King had a long chat with Rosella after the party.

'I am too old now,' he said with a sigh. 'I haven't decided yet who is going to have my kingdom after I die. I love all three of you equally. Whoever brings me the biggest treasure first will have my kingdom.'

'I promise father,' she said firmly. 'Luck is on my side. I will be the first.'

The next day Rosella asked one hundred witches and wizards to come with her and share her trip. They agreed. She ordered the preparation of one hundred black horses and one hundred magical crows for the long journey ahead.

When they left, it was an enchanted scene. One hundred witches and wizards galloped away down the path. Everyone was wearing black cloaks, pointy hats and black robes. One hundred black-as-night crows followed them into the darkness. They had one hundred magical glowing fire sticks to show them the way. Suddenly, the woods grew darker and darker and it was so impenetrable it was impossible to see anything. Only their magic could keep them going. They travelled for a long time: days, months or a year. Everybody got tired and ran out of energy. Suddenly, they saw an old abandoned black castle in the middle of the woods.

'I like this place,' said Rosella. 'It is enchanting. Let's build a new country down here and l will be the Queen. I will call it "The Darkness World".'

Everybody agreed and a new country was born. The Queen of The Darkness World completely forgot all about her promise.

Chapter 3

The days went by. It was time for Snowflake to have her 16th birthday party. She invited one hundred white snow fairies to celebrate. Everyone was wearing white, sparkly crystal dresses, tiaras and shiny ice skates. They had white marshmallows, cakes topped with white icing, vanilla ice cream, white ice lollies and white yoghurt during her party. They had an ice-skating ball after the meal and a spectacular fireworks finale. It was the most sparkly and white party the world had ever seen.

Straight after the party the king invited Snowflake to talk about her future.

'I told your sister a year ago,' said the King, 'whoever brings me the largest treasure first will have my kingdom. Go and bring me the treasure.'

'Yes, father. I promise. I will be the Queen,' she said gently.

Next morning, Snowflake took one hundred polar bears, one hundred snow fairies with white magic wands, one hundred snowy white doves and a few snow maids and snow kingsmen. It was an amazing sight when they all went past. The polar bears galloped away like horses with snow people on their backs. The snow fairies and doves flew beside them, like little snowy angels. They galloped and galloped for days and months. A thick blanket of snow fell on the ground. The snow storm was sticky, heavy and impenetrable.

It was freezing cold, but the bears kept running tirelessly through the snow. Finally, near the North Pole, Snowflake saw a large open area – perfect for a building.

'I would like to build a country down here,' Snowflake declared loudly. 'I will call my country Bearland,' she said proudly.

Snowflake declared herself to be the Queen and a new country was born. They were busy building the country with the help of magic and polar bears. The polar bears were good builders. Snowflake was so busy building, that she forgot all about the promise she had made to her father.

Chapter 4

Soon it was time to celebrate Mary's 16th birthday. She decided to organise the most colourful party the world had ever seen. It was a masquerade ball. Everyone had to choose their own unique colour for their outfit and magic up the most amazing ball gown. Colours were everywhere. Red, orange, pink, blue, indigo, magenta, yellow, golden and violet – lads and ladies danced around the ballroom. Mary also invited an orchestra of flamingos to play magical classical music throughout the magnificent ballroom. Then they had the most amazing colourful vegetable salads, multi-coloured finger food, strawberries, raspberries and kiwis.

After the party, the old King invited Mary for a private talk.

'As you know,' he said in his croaky voice, 'I am too old and might not survive much longer. Whoever of my magical daughters brings me the biggest treasure of all first, will receive my crown.'

'I will think about it,' Mary said with a smile and walked away.

Chapter 5

Next day, Mary ordered the unpacking of all her magical paintings and hang them around the castle. Then she invited her father to talk about the paintings.

'Look at all of these paintings I have created over the years. They are my biggest treasure. I give them to you as a gift.'

'Congratulations Mary!' said the King. You will be the next Queen of Philiphia.'

In a few days, the old King died. Everybody cried at his funeral.

Soon after, Mary organised a huge party to celebrate her coronation. She invited her sisters. They came and shared their stories. They were very proud of their own and each other's achievements.

The three Queens lived happily ever after.

The end of book 5